Bob Harkness is playing the role of protective son.

"He's taking advantage of your situation, Mom. Can't you see? You've just retired and don't know what direction you should take and a gray-haired knight in shining armor comes along and tries to sweep you off your feet."

Edith's eyes danced with anger. "Bob, that isn't exactly the way it happened. . . ."

"Let's approach it from a different angle. What kind of work did Roy do before he retired?"

"I've told you that he was a social worker."

"And what kind of income do retired social workers have?"

"I really haven't given it much thought. . . .He doesn't seem to have any overwhelming financial need, nor is he living extravagantly."

"But Mother, can't you see what he's interested in? It's a classic soap opera. I can't stand by and let a Prince Charming who is barely making an existence sweet-talk you out of all your savings. The money my father made belongs in the family, not to a fast-talking, gray-haired panther."

ANN BELL has worked as a teacher and librarian in schools in Iowa, Oregon, Guam, and Montana. Previously she has written numerous articles for Christian magazines and a study on the book of James.

Autumn
Love

Ann Bell

Heartsong Presents

For my mother, Frances Hartman, of Stuart, Iowa, who proofread this manuscript at age eighty-four; my children, Philip and Teresa Orr, who did not say, "But you're too old, Mother"; and my husband's children, Elizabeth Guimont, Pamela and Frances Bell, and Patricia Mishler, who did not say, "But not at your age, Dad."

ISBN 1-55748-453-8

AUTUMN LOVE

one

Biting March winds howled around the one-story high school building in central Montana. Yet the brick walls of Rocky Bluff High offered little protection from a more sinister threat as a loud, sharp report echoed down the lonely corridors. Edith Harkness ran from the teachers' lounge toward the principal's office as fast as her sixty-four-year-old legs could carry her. Montana born and bred, Edith was no stranger to guns and was an excellent shot herself. From the quickness of the resounding noise, she believed the offending weapon was a small-caliber handgun.

As she flung the office door open, the scene that greeted her filled her heart with terror. Her principal, Grady Walker, lay on the floor bleeding from a head wound. Viola Tomkins, his secretary, huddled in a corner crying hysterically. Edith instantly recognized the young man holding the .38 police special as Larry Reynolds, a tall, husky member of the senior class.

Edith felt her heart pound and blood rush to her face as though someone had slapped her on the cheek. She had to act quickly. Grady might survive if he could get to a hospital immediately.

First, however, she transferred her attention to Larry. He seemed detached from himself. Even though he was looking directly at her, he didn't show any recognition. *He's in a catatonic state*, she thought thankfully.

5

"Give me the gun, Larry." The confidence in her voice surprised her and she hoped Larry wouldn't see how frightened she was. The six-foot, two-inch quarterback of the Rocky Bluff football team, Larry was also the greatest center its basketball team had ever produced.

He pointed the gun at her chest.

"Larry," she said, taking a few steps toward him, "give me the gun and no one else will get hurt."

The young man's arm went limp. Gradually he relaxed his grip until the weapon fell into Edith's trembling hand. Within seconds she became aware of the crowd milling in the hallway outside the office door. Basketball coach Todd Watson pushed his way into the room.

"Todd, take Larry to your office. Hold him there until the police arrive."

"Come with me, Larry. Everything will be all right," the coach said soothingly as he led his player away. The crowd parted in shocked silence.

"Get the school nurse up here," Edith yelled to no one in particular. Yanking the telephone from its cradle, she dialed 911. "There has been a shooting at Rocky Bluff High School. We need an ambulance and the police immediately."

As Edith hung up the telephone, Amy Wallace, the school nurse, ran into the room. She immediately began to apply pressure to the principal's head in an effort to stop the bleeding.

Edith suddenly noticed she still had Larry's gun in her hand. Fighting the urge to fling it away, she took a deep breath and laid the weapon on the principal's desk.

A boost of adrenalin seemed to surge through her as she pulled the trembling secretary to her feet. Still sobbing, Viola laid her head on Edith's shoulder.

"Amy, can you handle Grady by yourself?" Edith questioned anxiously as she supported most of Viola's weight against her body.

"Yes. Get Viola out of here."

Edith turned Viola over to the the physical education teacher who took her to the teachers' lounge. She then quietly made her way to her own classroom past a curious crowd of onlooking faculty and students. She fell into her chair, buried her head into her hands, and cried. Her heart continued to pound uncontrollably and she was having trouble breathing. As the ambulance sirens became louder, she fought to compose herself. Help was on the way!

A short time later Amy burst into the room accompanied by a police officer. "Edith, are you all right?"

"Yes, I think so. How is Grady?"

"He's one lucky man. The bullet grazed his temple and caused a lot of bleeding, but he'll be fine in a few days. They're taking him to the hospital for observation. Edith, this officer wants to ask you some questions and afterward I want to check you over."

Edith spoke into the officer's pocket-sized tape recorder, trying to describe exactly what happened. She agonized over every detail of those terrifying moments. In retelling the story she was surprised at how fast it had happened. She was in the office no more than two minutes, but those moments had seemed like an eternity.

After the officer left Edith walked down the corridor

to the nurse's office where Amy waited. "Lie down on the cot," Amy directed as Edith nearly collapsed onto the clean sheets. "I want to check your pulse and blood pressure."

A worried frown spread across Amy's face. "Do you have a history of heart trouble, Edith?"

"No, I rarely even have a cold."

"Any member of your family ever had heart trouble?"

"Not that I know of. I lost my husband to a heart attack ten years ago but there was no history of heart trouble in his family either. Why do you ask?"

"Well, your pulse rate is sky high and your blood pressure is almost off the charts. This is most likely a reaction to the horrible experience you had today, but to be on the safe side, I'd like a doctor to examine you."

"I'm sure I'll be okay, but if you think it's necessary I'll go."

"I'll call Dr. Brewer and tell him it's an emergency. Classes are dismissed for the rest of the day. See the doctor and then go straight home. Better yet, take several days off work. I'll call you tomorrow."

Edith returned to her classroom and mechanically took her purse from the top left-hand drawer and her coat from the closet. The bitter cold wind didn't bother her as she walked across the parking lot. She was already numb with shock.

Cautiously she steered the car down Grove Street to Dr. Brewer's office. The nurse quickly ushered her into an examining room, bypassing patients already waiting in the reception area.

"Edith, you have the heart of a twenty year old," the dark-haired, middle-aged doctor assured her after he completed a few minutes of routine examination. "Your elevated blood pressure is merely due to the crisis you experienced. I'll write a prescription for a tranquilizer to help you rest tonight."

"Dr. Brewer, I've never taken a tranquilizer in my life and I'm not about to start now," Edith stated firmly. "If it is all right with you I'd just as soon take a couple aspirin and have a cup of herbal tea to help me relax. It has worked for me before, I don't know why it wouldn't work tonight."

The doctor considered a moment. "Go ahead, try the aspirin and tea, but be sure and call me if you have any problems. I do want you to take a few days off work, though."

That evening Edith's daughter-in-law Nancy came to visit. The two women relaxed in the living room. Nancy curled her long, slender legs under her on the sofa while Edith leaned back in her recliner by the window.

"Bob would be here but he's in Billings buying inventory for the store," Nancy said. "Jay and Dawn send their love. They wanted to come but I didn't want them out late on a school night."

"I can't erase those few horrible moments from my mind," Edith confessed with her hand still trembling as she took a sip of tea. "I keep asking myself why. Why Larry Reynolds? Why here in Rocky Bluff?"

"Mom, the Reynoldses are good customers at the store, but all I know about Larry is that he's the community sports hero."

Edith lifted her shoulders helplessly. "Larry is more than a good athlete. As the kids say, he's a megastar.

He was quarterback of the football team, but his greatest talent was on the basketball floor. Everybody admired him. Larry has had more press coverage than anyone else in the history of Rocky Bluff."

"Sounds like he earned it."

"Yes, he has," Edith explained. "For two years running he was named center on the all-state basketball team. To top off his outstanding high school career, last month he received a basketball scholarship to Montana A & M."

"He had everything going for him. Why would he throw it all away now?"

"Actually he threw it away two weeks ago. Remember when half the town went to Billings to see the Class A State Basketball Championship? I yelled myself hoarse. I was proud of our school and even prouder of our basketball team, especially Larry. He did an outstanding job."

"Bob listened to the game on the radio," Nancy recalled with an amused grin. "I've never heard him get that excited over a simple ball game. The next day there were rumors around town that some of the team got in trouble after the game. What happened?"

"As I understand it, after the game the team went out to celebrate, and a few of the boys had a little too much to drink, Larry among them. On the way back to the motel Larry was stopped by the Billings police for running a red light and was given a breathalizer test. He was well over the legal limit. To make matters worse, at his booking the police found three marijuana cigarettes in his shirt pocket."

Nancy's mouth dropped open with surprise. "I've

heard of drug problems in Great Falls and Billings but not here in Rocky Bluff."

"We've been fortunate until now," Edith explained. "As far as I know this was the first time any of our students were involved with drugs. Rocky Bluff could have forgiven him for the DUI, but not for the marijuana. Grady had no choice but to suspend him for the remainder of the school year."

"But isn't Larry a senior? Wouldn't that affect his graduation in June?"

"Worse than that, he not only won't graduate in June, but Montana A & M cancelled his basketball scholarship. His parents can't afford to send him to college without that scholarship. Larry blamed Grady for all his problems and vowed revenge."

"It sounds like he just snapped under the pressure," Nancy observed.

Edith hesitated a moment. "That is the sad commentary on small town athletics. We put too much pressure on our young people to perform well and entertain us. Larry simply could not handle it."

"The ones I feel sorry for are Larry's parents. They are in the store nearly every week picking up supplies for their ranch. They appear to be such hard-working people who would sacrifice anything for their children. They also have a son in the third grade with Jay. All he can talk about is his big brother."

"Bob gave me cause for many sleepless nights during his high school days. But he outgrew his rebellious nature," Edith confessed to her daughter-in-law. "During his school days alcohol was the biggest temptation to the students, and that was generally limited to an occasional Saturday night beer party."

"Oh, look at the time," Nancy groaned, glancing at her watch. "If I don't do a load of laundry tonight the family won't have any clothes to wear tomorrow. I'll stop by in the morning and see how you're doing. Have a good night's sleep."

Nancy leaned over and kissed her mother-in-law on the forehead before slipping out the door into the late winter evening.

Edith sat in silence for a few minutes trying to calm her racing heart. She reached for her Bible on the coffee table beside her and turned to her favorite passage, the twenty-third Psalm.

> *The LORD is my shepherd; I shall not want.*
>
> *He maketh me to lie down in green pastures: he leadeth me beside the still waters.*
>
> *He restoreth my soul: he leadeth me in the paths of righteousness for his name's sake.*
>
> *Yea, though I walk through the valley of the shadow of death, I will fear no evil: for thou art with me; thy rod and thy staff they comfort me.*
>
> *Thou preparest a table before me in the presence of mine enemies: thou anointest my head with oil; my cup runneth over.*
>
> *Surely goodness and mercy shall follow me all the days of my life: and I will dwell in the house of the LORD for ever.*

Edith tried to pray but words escaped her. Surely the Lord heard her heartfelt cry, for Grady . . . for Larry . . .for herself. She laid her Bible on the coffee table and walked slowly to the kitchen phone. If ever she needed a human voice to talk to it was now.

She dialed the familiar number in Chamberland, Idaho, and waited for her daughter Jean to answer. Upon hearing the familiar "Hello" Edith broke down and sobbed.

"Mother, what's wrong?"

Edith regained her composure. "Honey, the most terrible thing happened today. One of our students shot the principal, and I happened to be the one to take the loaded gun away from him. I was absolutely terrified and I still haven't stopped shaking."

"Mother! Tell me exactly what happened."

Edith retold the story. As the words tumbled out, her heart raced.

"I wish I could be there with you tonight," Jean moaned. "You shouldn't be alone after such an experience."

"I'll be fine," Edith tried to assure her with false sincerity. "I've already decided what I am going to do."

"What's that?"

"Tomorrow I'm going to turn in my resignation effective at the end of this school year. I will be sixty-five in a few weeks and I have an ample income from the store. I need to get away from the school, away from Rocky Bluff. What kind of world is it where school children try to kill their principals, or even their teachers? I survived a terrible ordeal and I don't ever want another experience like that."

"Mom, why don't you wait a few days before deciding something so important? Things may look better in a few days."

"No, Jean, my mind is made up. I want to retire to Arizona where many of my friends are. I can still maintain controlling interest in the hardware store from there. Bob is doing a good job managing its daily affairs. In fact, he appears to resent anything I do regarding the store. He seems to have forgotten that his father and I ran that store successfully for over thirty years."

"I know you've worked hard all your life and deserve a rest, but I wish you would wait a while before you make definite plans."

"I appreciate your concern, but I know what I have to do." Edith was too tired to argue and steered the conversation to the antics of Jay and Dawn. They chatted aimlessly for a full ten minutes before hanging up.

Extremely tired now, Edith went into her bedroom and laid out her nightgown. She then went to the bathroom and filled the tub. As she was undressing the telephone rang.

"Oh, no!" she groaned. "Who could that be at this hour?"

"Mom!" Bob's rapid-fire delivery followed, the trademark of this consummate business professional. "I'm still in Billings. Nancy called and told me what happened. Are you sure you're all right?"

"I'm fine. Just very tired. I'm getting ready to take a bath and go to bed."

"It must have been a frightening day. You don't need any more experiences like that."

"That's the understatement of the year," Edith sighed

as she sank into the chair beside the phone.

"You know, Mom, you've worked hard all your life. Why not think about retiring? The Millers and several of your other friends have moved to Arizona. Why don't you join them?"

"I've been thinking about doing that very thing. In fact, I'm going to turn in my resignation to the assistant principal tomorrow. If I move to Sun City I can still be in telephone contact with you as to the operation of the store."

"Mom, I don't think you even need the worry of the store. Why don't you turn the operation completely over to Nancy and me and save yourself the worries?"

"The business arrangement we have right now is working very well. You run the day-to-day routine and I'll make the major decisions. Your father and I started that store from scratch thirty years ago, and it wouldn't be what it is today if it hadn't been for your father's hard work."

"But things are changing so rapidly. It will be hard for you to keep up from the sidelines. You deserve a rest."

Edith's irritation rose. "If I leave teaching I'll have even more time to devote to the store, not less."

"Mother, why do you want that extra worry?" Bob persisted. "You will have enough income to live comfortably wherever you choose. You deserve a break after all you've been through. You're almost sixty-five. You don't need to be working with deranged youth who run around using guns on their teachers. There are plenty of younger teachers to handle the misfits of today."

"That was the conclusion I was coming to myself. I was very disappointed with the younger teachers today. They all just stood there frozen with fear. It seemed like none of them knew what to do. I was never so glad to see a familiar face over fifty as I was to see Coach Watson."

"Today you were competent, but you're getting too old to keep up with all the changes in the *business* world."

Edith's eyes fired with rage. "Bob, soon I may be too old to handle deranged young people, but I'm not too old to handle my own business affairs. That is not open for further discussion."

"I didn't mean to upset you, Mother," Bob stated with an air of condescension. "You are tired and need to get some rest. I'll see you in a couple days."

Edith hung up the phone and took a deep breath. The crisis of the day had been more than she wanted to deal with. She didn't want to end it with a conflict with her son. The tub of warm water filled with soothing bath oils was inviting.

He maketh me to lie down in green pastures, he leadeth me beside the still waters, Edith recited to herself as she relaxed in the bath. As the tensions of the day began to leave her body, she was able to put her future plans—and her disagreement with Bob—into perspective. I want to retire from teaching...but I'm not too old to be a contributing member of society!

two

"But Grady, isn't there any way I can get my teaching position back?" Edith protested as she surveyed the handsome, dark-haired principal. "It's only been three weeks since I turned in my resignation and left for a vacation in Arizona. Resigning was the most foolish thing I've ever done."

"I questioned the wisdom of it at the time. But you were so shaken over the episode with Larry Reynolds that nothing would change your mind."

"My daughter tried to discourage me from acting so quickly, but back then I was determined to get as far away from here as possible."

"I'm sorry it turned out this way, but it is out of my hands now," Grady Walker explained as apologetically as he could. "Two days after you submitted your resignation to the school board they received an application from a home economics teacher in Vermont who wanted to relocate to Montana. She has her master's degree and twelve years of experience. The school board was so impressed with her credentials and her enthusiasm that they offered her a contract on the spot."

"I was so sure before I left for spring break that I wanted to retire and move. But I should never have submitted my resignation prematurely. I didn't know how much the people of Rocky Bluff meant to me until I was away and realized that I would be giving up everything I cherished the most."

17

"I sympathize with your situation," the principal tried to assure her, "but I'm sure in a few months you'll be glad you retired when you did. You're still strong and healthy enough to do all the things you have wanted to do for years."

Edith thanked him and walked gloomily back to her classroom. She had assumed her position would still be open and she could continue teaching for a couple more years. She wasn't ready to retire.

Rocky Bluff High School had been good to her. Few school districts would have been willing to hire a fifty-five-year-old widow who was returning to teaching after a twenty-five-year layoff. Because of their confidence in her potential, Edith had worked hard not to disappoint them. However, now faced with the finality of her resignation letter, a sense of fear kept tugging at the back of her brain. All her life she had been needed; she did not feel ready to join her older friends in Sun City.

She felt she had to share her frustrations with someone. Even though her relationship with Bob was strained, Edith decided to confide in him when he got off work at the family hardware store that evening.

"But Mom," Bob protested as Edith explained her decision not to retire to Sun City after all. "I thought you had it all worked out to turn complete ownership and control of the store over to me and retire south. Why would you want to stay in Rocky Bluff, especially when the school board has already hired a replacement for you?"

"At your age I know it's hard to understand, but I don't feel sixty-five. Seeing my retired friends passing their days by playing golf, bridge, and chess I knew

I could never resign myself to that kind of life. I thought maybe I could help part-time at the store by keeping the books. I know your present bookkeeper wants more time off to spend with her family."

"Things have changed since you were the primary bookkeeper for Dad. You know we've completely computerized our bookkeeping system. It's a totally different world today."

"Bob, I can always learn new skills. Every quarter they offer computer classes at the community college. Many people my age have been taking them. Besides, Nancy said she would teach me your particular system."

Edith was becoming more and more frustrated as the conversation progressed. Little had she realized when she turned the actual management of the store over to Bob after George's death that she would be frozen out even though she was still the legal owner of the business. Bob did not want her back at the store in any capacity and the conversation was going nowhere. She turned and walked away. Tension filled the room.

"Mother, don't go away angry," Bob called after her. "I'm sure there are other things you can do to pass your time in Rocky Bluff."

Edith did not respond and let the door slam behind her as she left.

Seeing no immediate solution to her imminent retirement, Edith resolved to ignore the pressure from her son and continue her normal routine. The last few weeks of school flew by with the usual end-of-the-year activities. As senior class sponsor she was busy planning the senior picnic, senior-parent brunch, and graduation.

The reality of her retirement hit her on the last day of school.

"Goodbye, have a good summer," Edith responded to her last student's farewell. Edith shuffled restlessly to her desk. This was not the end of a typical school year, this was the end of her teaching career. *I wish I hadn't submitted my resignation so early,* she lamented for the thousandth time. *I have only myself to blame. I should have waited.*

"Your end-of-the-year reports seem in order, Edith," Grady Walker observed, glancing over the attendance and grade sheets. "I realize it must be extremely difficult to hand me the key to the home economics room for the last time. You've invested ten years of your life developing an outstanding program and the school is extremely grateful for your contributions."

Edith's mind began to roam as the principal expounded about her accomplishments and the many students who entered the working world better prepared because of her dedication. *"Difficult to hand in the key" is the biggest understatement of the year,* she thought. *I now have nothing to do with my time and am no longer needed anywhere. Even my own son doesn't want me to work at the very store his father and I founded.*

"As interested as you've been in all aspects of community affairs, you must have some exciting retirement plans," Grady continued, bringing Edith's wandering mind back to the present.

"Not really," Edith replied, trying to shove her inner feelings into the background. "I plan to get my garden planted right away and then spend a couple weeks in

Idaho with my daughter Jean."

"I wish you the very best," he declared, rising from his vinyl padded office chair and escorting her to the door. "Do stop back and see us from time to time."

No mention was made of the encounter with Larry Reynolds and the gun. The situation was still too painful for both of them to discuss.

"Thank you" was all Edith could utter through the lump building in her throat. She hurried down the hallway for the last time, tears cascading down her cheeks.

The hot May sun beat down on the cement parking lot as Edith blindly found her way to her Ford Escort. Fumbling in her black leather purse, she took out her sunglasses and keys and dabbed her eyes and face with a lone tissue. Solemnly inserting the key into the lock she opened the door and slid mechanically behind the wheel. All her habits of the last ten years were about to end. The drive onto Grove Street and then Main took on a strange new meaning. Ever since she had come to Rocky Bluff as a new bride she had felt a part of the lifeblood of the community. Today that part of her life was over.

In front of the county courthouse Edith's serious face relaxed and the corners of her mouth turned up. Skipping down the sidewalk was her six-year-old granddaughter. Carefully, Edith pulled into a vacant parking stall as Dawn came darting toward the familiar car.

"Hi, Grandma, are you glad that school's out?" Dawn shouted. "I am," she continued without waiting for a response.

"Hello, sweetie," Edith replied as she quickly joined her granddaughter on the sidewalk. "I'm sad that school is over," she explained, putting her arm around the child's slim shoulders. "I'll never be going back like you will be."

"I wish I didn't have to. Can I come home with you, instead of going to the babysitter's?"

Later that night as Edith was curled up in her favorite chair reading the current *Better Homes and Gardens* the phone rang.

"Mom, do you have your garden in yet?" Jean questioned with characteristic eagerness as Edith greeted her. "When are you coming to visit us?"

"Jean, you haven't changed in the least. You never forget a 'maybe' promise," Edith teased. "I just finished teaching school six hours ago and my superhuman abilities do not lend themselves to planting the garden today."

"Since you've confessed your mortality, I'll give you until a week from Friday to get your garden in order and then Jim and I will meet the seven P.M. bus from Rocky Bluff."

"Seriously, Jean, are you sure I won't be in the way? You and Jim both work and have been so busy lately."

"Mother, don't be silly. Of course you won't be in the way. I know it will be rather lonesome during the daytime, but we'll make up for it in the evenings and weekends," Jean replied, ignoring her mother's weak protests. As a hospital nurse she had developed a sensitivity to both the spoken and the unspoken needs of others. "Once you get here I know you'll find more than enough things to do. I might even give you some mending."

"You've convinced me," Edith said enthusiastically. "But please, no more hemming cheerleader skirts. I gave that up the day you graduated."

"I promise," Jean replied. Then a note of seriousness entered her voice. "In fact, I thought we'd do some sightseeing next Saturday and go to the symphony that night. There is a lot of beautiful country to see, and a symphonic orchestra from Seattle will be in town for that weekend."

"That sounds great," Edith readily agreed. She switched the phone to the other ear, pushing aside wisps of her gray-flecked black hair. She enjoyed classical music and professional symphonies rarely toured in Rocky Bluff, Montana.

Friday morning Edith boarded the Trailways bus. Although she was eager to see her daughter and son-in-law, who hadn't been home to Rocky Bluff in nearly a year, a sense of fear and doubt began to plague her. *Will I be able to develop an independent lifestyle, or will I become a dependent old woman?* she pondered. *Does Jean really miss those talks we used to have or is she just patronizing me? After all, she's a grown, married woman now, more capable than I to deal with the problems of life.*

As the bus turned off the interstate and headed toward the business section of Chamberland, Edith fell into a peaceful silence, lost in her own thoughts.

A block from the Chamberland station she spied Jean and Jim standing outside the depot. The young couple's fingers were entwined in simple unity. How often she and George had enjoyed that same sense of oneness! Immersing herself in the lives of high school students had not replaced the empty place at the dinner table, or the gentle snoring in her bed. Rarely could she look upon a happily married couple without feeling a twinge of emptiness, but it was even more acute when she saw the shared love of her own daughter and son-in-law. *Was it time to pass the torch of happiness and usefulness on to the next generation?* she thought as she gathered her packages around her.

"Mom, I'm glad you could come," Jean exclaimed as she gave her mother a warm embrace. "Jim will get your luggage for you. How was your trip? Have you had dinner yet?"

"No, we didn't have a long enough stop at any of the towns along the way, and I'm famished." Edith handed Jim her claim check, relieved to have a man around to help with the heavy suitcases.

"There's a new Chinese restaurant at the edge of town. Let's go there for dinner. We have so much visiting to catch up on." Jean happily led the way through the maze of cars in the parking lot.

A petite, dark-haired hostess dressed in a Chinese-style embroidered robe and slippers led the party of three to a private back table. A few minutes later after perusing the menu, the only item they all understood was the eggroll. Their confused expressions summoned the waitress who patiently described each dish on the menu. After much deliberation Edith chose chow mai fon with pork while Jean and Jim decided upon Szechwan beef with scallions.

They barely had time to discuss the recent events of the sawmill that Jim managed when the waitress returned with the meal and chopsticks. After several hilarious attempts, the chopsticks were abandoned for the knife and fork. The food and atmosphere complemented the family news each wanted to share.

"Mother, have you thought about how you're going to spend your time now that you have more of it?" Jim asked, taking a sip of orange pekoe tea. "I don't mean to pry, but more than anything I want to see you happy."

"I'm not sure yet," Edith responded hesitantly. "My garden will keep me busy most of the summer. Then the house will need plenty of tender loving care. It hasn't had a thorough cleaning since your father passed away. I piled all his tools and personal belongings in the storage room in the basement and have rarely opened the door since then. I've been so busy with the young people at school that I've kept putting off that job."

"All your work projects might keep you busy until Christmas, but then what? Have you thought about working part-time at the hardware store with Bob?"

Edith's eyes became distant. *Is this a good time to explain the hurtful truth? Should I let Jean know that all is not well between her brother and me?* She took a sip of tea before she answered.

"Jean, you don't know how much I'd like to work at the store. I'd enjoy taking computer classes at the community college to learn to use the new business computer software," Edith explained, laying her fork on her plate and concentrating on every word, "but I'm afraid that Bob would resent my presence."

"But why, Mom?" Jean had a look of bewilderment in her eyes. "What's happened to my easy-going, fun-loving brother?"

"I don't fully understand myself. Bob seems to think when a person reaches age sixty-five both the mind and body cease to function."

"That kind of thinking has forced society to change its policy toward a retirement based solely on chronological age," Jim said with irritation in his voice.

"Mom, that brings us back to the first question. Despite what Bob thinks, you deserve a meaningful retirement life. What are you going to do with your time? You're not ready to settle back in your rocking chair all day long."

"That's something I'm still working on." Edith's suppressed restlessness was beginning to surface. "I didn't think retirement would affect me this way. I enjoy stopping at the senior citizens center for a cup of coffee now and then and visiting with friends, but I can't spend all my time doing that. I can't get interested in playing bridge or canasta or cribbage, and I'd rather curl up with a good book than play bingo. If others enjoy that sort of recreation, that's fine, but it's just not for me."

The days with Jean and Jim passed swiftly. Each new day brought long walks in the park and time to enjoy one another's company. There were visits over the back fence with Jean's neighbor, and time to read the top three books on the nonfiction best-seller list. Edith never had another twinge of not being needed, but after two weeks she was ready to return to her own home and garden.

Edith's period of mental escape ended as she boarded the morning bus bound for Rocky Bluff the last Friday of June. One concern weighed heavy on her mind, one that would not be resolved in a few hours. How could she convince her son that Harkness Hardware was a *family* business and not solely *his* business? What would she do with herself for the rest of her life?

three

"Welcome home, Grandma," Jay and Dawn shouted as Edith stepped off the bus at the Rocky Bluff station. "We missed you a lot."

Edith grabbed both grandchildren and pulled them against her. "I missed you too. As soon as we get my suitcases I have some special surprises for each of you."

"Mom, you certainly have a way of spoiling those kids," Nancy teased as she gave her mother-in-law a warm hug. "It's good to have you home."

"I'm glad to be back. But for the record, my grandchildren are not spoiled, they're just well loved."

Nancy giggled while Edith's eyes scanned the bus terminal. "Didn't Bob come with you?" she queried with a note of disappointment in her voice.

"I've afraid not. He's busy working on the books at the store. He said he'd be by to see you Sunday afternoon."

"Well, this is Friday night, our traditional family night," Edith sighed as she took Dawn's hand and walked toward the baggage counter. Not wanting her grandchildren to be suspicious of the tension between their father and his mother, she quickly changed the subject. "But the four of us can still make it a special occasion. Let's stop at the Dairy Queen for ice cream on our way home."

The Thursday before school started passed with the usual late summer flurry of activities. Edith paused a moment at the basement window. Jay and Dawn were happily constructing what they called a clubhouse from the pile of scrap lumber George had left stacked behind the garage. Suddenly an idea flashed through her mind. "Jay, Dawn, put your tools away and come with me. I need your help."

"Where are we going, Grandma?" Jay wondered, his sandy hair in its usual disarray as a cool breeze whistled through the trees. Without waiting for an answer Dawn and Jay hurriedly gathered up the hammers and nails and piled them on the workbench in the garage and came running to the house as fast as their legs would carry them.

"I've decided to paint my house and I need your help in picking out the colors. Let's surprise your parents and go to the store as ordinary customers."

As she drove her grandchildren down the tree-lined streets of Rocky Bluff, Edith's countenance changed. *What colors do I want in my bedroom, or in my kitchen and living room?* she pondered. Instead of a future vagueness concerning her day-to-day routine after the children returned to school, she now knew what Monday morning would bring. Dressed in her faded blue jeans, she would be wielding a paintbrush, thankful that she still had the physical strength to maintain her own home.

Edith's feelings of anticipation were momentarily dampened when her son learned of her plans. "Now Mother, are you sure you can paint the inside of the house by yourself? I've a good friend who could use the work, and he'll be finished with his construction site job sometime next month," Bob volunteered as Edith and the children thumbed through the sample cards of available paint.

"No, Bob, I want to get it done right away," she insisted, angered at the subtle questioning of her abilities. "The last time the walls were painted was when your father did it fifteen years ago, and I'm ready for a change. Why should I pay someone else to do it when I have the time and can probably do as good a job as they?"

"I still think you should call Ron Brown. You've worked hard all your life and deserve a rest."

"You don't seem to understand. This is something I want to do myself. It may take me a little longer, but at least I'll have the satisfaction of accomplishment."

"Well, if you insist, Mother, I won't stand in your way. Just remember you aren't as young as you used to be."

"But I'm not ready for a rocking chair either," Edith replied stubbornly.

"What color are you going to paint your living room, Grandma?" Jay interrupted as he glanced through the pile of paint samples. "I like the lime green."

"You have good taste, Jay. Maybe if we paint it one shade darker it will match the carpet better. Then we can paint the ceiling white to add more light to the room."

Edith turned her attention back to her overbearing son standing behind the counter. A mixture of anger and pity engulfed her. If only he would try to understand her situation. In a brisk businesslike manner she instructed, "Just have your delivery person bring the sample number 24 green paint and sample number 5 white paint along with two rollers, two brushes for the trim, two paint pans, and three sheets of plastic to the house before the store closes tomorrow. I want to begin in the living room as soon as possible."

Edith didn't let her son's words and attitude dishearten her for long. The next morning the children helped Edith move the furniture and together they began putting masking tape around the windows and the trim in the living room. Dawn was proud of the way she covered the carpeting with newspapers. When the painting materials arrived later in the day, they had finished preparing the room.

"I'm ready to start painting and you're both ready to go back to school, so let's celebrate," Edith said to her grandchildren as they surveyed their hard work. "Let's go out for banana splits. It's my treat for a job well done. I wouldn't have been done until late tonight if you both hadn't helped."

"I wish I didn't have to go to school tomorrow so I could help you paint. It looks like a lot of fun," Jay declared as he reached for his baseball cap and followed his sister out the door.

"I'm sorry you won't be able to help but school comes first. However, as soon as I'm finished I'm going to invite you to my celebration party."

By ten the next evening Edith had completed the first coat of paint on the living room wall and fell into bed exhausted. *When I finish painting in the living room, maybe I'll shampoo the carpeting,* she thought as her eyes closed. Edith drifted into a deep sleep and did not stir until the morning sun shone directly into her bedroom.

The next few days followed the same basic pattern. The former home economics teacher budgeted her strength and maintained a steady work pattern. By late the following Friday the furniture, pictures, and knickknacks were back in place. Edith picked up the telephone and called Harkness Hardware.

"Hello, Nancy," she greeted. "I've finished painting the downstairs and shampooing the carpeting and I figure it's time for a celebration. How about you and Bob bringing the children over for Sunday dinner? I'll be sure and make your favorite dishes."

"We'd love to, Mom. Is there anything I can bring?"

"This is entirely my treat. Just bring your appetites and nothing more."

Sunday Edith hurried home from church in order to put the finishing touches on dinner before her guests arrived. Soon she heard familiar footsteps on the porch.

"Mom, this is beautiful," Nancy admired as she stepped into the freshly painted living room. "You've done an excellent job. It's as good as any professional could have done."

Edith smiled to herself as she intentionally avoided looking her son in the eye. She had learned long ago never to say I told you so.

"Thanks, dear. After painting the walls and cleaning the carpet don't you think the drapes look a bit shabby?" Edith asked as she critically surveyed her windows. "How about taking a couple hours off work Monday to help me pick out new drapes?"

"That sounds like fun. I'll meet you at one at

Herman's Drapery."

Bob didn't want his mother's momentary victory to go unchecked. He walked around the living room then cleared his throat. "I must admit, Mother, that you did a good job, but I still think you'll need help with the upstairs bedrooms. Those high slanting ceilings could be dangerous. You'll need more than a stepladder to do the job safely. I'll call Ron Brown in the morning, that is, if you'd like."

"You'll do nothing of the sort. Beverly Short from next door said she'd come over and help me when I get to the hard part. She even has some scaffolding from her husband's old carpentry business."

"But Beverly is nearly seventy," Bob protested, speaking to his mother the way he did to his own children. "What if one of you falls off the ladder and breaks a leg? I'd never forgive myself for letting you do your own painting."

"We could break a leg walking down our front steps too. Neither situation has anything to do with you. The subject is closed. I'll finish the painting myself." Edith placed her hands firmly on her hips and stomped into the kitchen. Nancy shot a look of annoyance at her husband who was shaking his head in frustration. Without a word she followed her mother-in-law into the kitchen.

The subject of who was to paint the house was not discussed again. Despite how old and feeble she might become, Edith never wanted to be mothered by her own children. Whenever she needed more supplies from the hardware store she waited until Nancy was free to help her.

The week before Thanksgiving Edith completed painting the interior of her house. For several minutes after the last paint can was carried to the garage she wandered throughout her home admiring the change of tone and mood. In a sense it was symbolic of a change of direction she wanted her life to take. Yet it would take more than a can of paint to change her unsettled future. As she took a cup of coffee and relaxed on her living room couch, a sense of loneliness swept over her.

If only George were here to share my moment of triumph. . . . Now Edith, she scolded herself, *there's no reason to sit here sulking. You are surrounded by a host of friends and neighbors. Invite them over to share your happiness.*

The next Wednesday afternoon the Harkness home was a hive of activity as a dozen neighbors noisily approved Edith's and Bev's hard work. After a tour of the house, some visiting, and coffee, punch, and strawberry rhubarb dessert, one by one the guests asked for their coats and bade the hostess farewell. As the door closed behind the last group, only one neighbor remained.

"Edith, now that you're not working full time would you be interested in joining our Ladies Aid group?" Grace Blair, a friend who lived in the next block, asked hesitantly. "We meet the first and third Tuesdays of every month and we'd love to have you join us."

"I'd be delighted to."

"Great, I'll pick you up Tuesday at one-fifteen," Grace said breezily as she reached for her coat. "I'm sure you'll enjoy it. We are quite an active group of women."

Tuesday afternoon Edith was standing at the window as Grace pulled her Chevy Citation to the curb in front of the house. She grabbed her coat and hurried to the waiting car. After exchanging greetings Edith was full of questions concerning the group's activities. In her heart Edith was hoping that the rumors about the center of community gossip were unfounded.

When Grace hesitated before answering, Edith sensed she was caught off-balance. "Every Christmas we send a basket of goodies to the nursing home," Grace began, evidently surprised that someone as active in the church as Edith didn't know about the activities of the Ladies Aid.

Not satisfied, Edith persisted. "Do you run the nursery? Serve church dinners? Support the missionaries? Help at the rescue mission? Have Bible study groups?"

Grace again hesitated, then cleared her throat. "It's kind of hard to explain," she replied as she slowed for the stoplight. "We're a pretty small group to make much of an impact on the needs of the community. Basically we just enjoy getting together and sharing each other's company."

Imagine a church group not having a purpose, Edith pondered as Grace parked the car in the church parking lot. *Maybe Grace is so involved in the group that she no longer realizes how ineffective it is.*

Grace and Edith descended the stairs to the basement and quietly slipped into the waiting chairs as the chairwoman finished the opening prayer. Ellen Watson then read Hebrews 11 and asked if there were any discussion over the chapter. The room was silent as each of the eight women looked at one another and then at the floor.

"If there is no discussion, let's go on with the business meeting," Ellen continued. "Is there any old business?"

Again the room fell silent, except for the chiming of the wall clock in the background. "Is there any new business?" Ellen's voice again echoed against the blank walls as everyone looked at the floor. The leader's eyes swept the room. "I'd like to welcome our guest, Edith Harkness. I hope she'll be able to join us on a regular basis."

Edith smiled as each woman in turn gave her a warm greeting. When the room was again quiet Ellen continued. "If there is no business, who will be responsible for refreshments for the next meeting when we'll be assembling our Christmas baskets?"

At that point the group seemed to come alive. "Oh, I'll be glad to do that," Betty volunteered, before anyone else had a chance to respond. "I found an excellent recipe for cherry turnovers in my mother's old cookbook."

"That sounds delicious. Does it use the regular pie crust recipe?" Grace inquired, adjusting her wire-framed glasses on her nose.

"Not quite. It calls for a half-cup more flour and a little more salt than what I use for my pumpkin pies." Cooking had long been Betty's favorite pastime, a skill advertised by her own ample figure.

"Not to change the subject," Joy piped in with her high twangy voice, "but did you taste Hilda's pie at the last potluck supper? I don't know what she did to it, but I would've been embarrassed to have brought anything like that to a church dinner."

"Yes, I did notice the bland flavor and lack of spices. But maybe we shouldn't judge Hilda too severely," Ellen protested, trying to regain her authority. "You know that her husband has divorced her to marry Kay Bly. It must've been very traumatic for her and she's just not up to her normal self."

"Oh, poor dear," Helen cooed, her eyes shining with interest. "I never did think much of him. He never stayed home with Hilda and the children. She had to raise their family almost entirely by herself."

"Well, maybe we should all pray for them instead of discussing their personal problems," Ellen tried to remind them.

"I didn't know all this was happening to poor Hilda," Grace inserted. "I really don't know how to pray for her. Maybe you can share more of the details so I can pray intelligently."

With each added comment Edith became more and more withdrawn and angered. She did not want to participate or spend her time in idle gossip disguised as Christian concern. Maybe someday she could help start a more meaningful group, but she had had enough for now.

During Thanksgiving vacation Edith decided to attack her long overdue task of sorting through the basement storage room. At least her time in the cluttered basement would accomplish more than watching morning soap operas. Besides, Jay and Dawn were coming that afternoon and they could help her load the boxes into the car.

As she cautiously opened the door of the storage room, a flood of memories engulfed her and she was enveloped by a wave of guilt for her own procrastination. George would have wanted this done long ago so that others could make use of his things. With a deep breath and a sudden surge of determination, Edith began sorting through the boxes.

When the children arrived that afternoon, Edith led them to the basement. "Would you help carry these things to the car for me? They were your grandfather's and I want to take them to the Salvation Army so that others may use them."

As soon as the door opened, Dawn spied her grandfather's old golf clubs in the corner. "Did Grandpa play golf?"

"Oh, yes. For many years every Sunday afternoon your grandpa and I would tee off in a foursome with the Millers. They moved to Arizona soon after your grandpa died, and I haven't touched a golf club since."

"Do you want this old shovel carried to the car too?" Jay asked, picking up the rusty tool leaning against the wall.

"I don't have any use for it now. Your grandfather used that a great deal when he was helping level the ground for the city park. The young people who play there today will never know all the sweat and toil that went into building that park."

Dawn continued exploring the once forbidden room. "What did Grandpa do to earn this trophy?" she asked, picking the brass statue from the top of a pasteboard box.

Edith smiled with satisfaction as she remembered how George was honored as the outstanding businessman of 1968. The children were learning more about their grandfather by helping clean the storage room than by all the stories their father had told them. "I was very proud of your grandfather as he walked across the stage to receive that award. The president of the Rocky Bluff Rotary Club acknowledged his contributions to many community affairs."

Taking the treasured trophy from Dawn, Edith placed it in a box she was saving and picked up George's black leather Bible. The edges were tattered and torn and the binding was broken. Gently she flipped the pages. Edith paused long enough to read some of the passages he had underlined in red ink. One by one the children came to look over her shoulder.

"See all the words underlined in red? Your grandfather wanted to indicate every verse that meant something to him. He loved God and he left his family with a name that you can be proud to carry on."

Dawn wrapped her arms around her grandmother's neck. "If Grandpa was anything like you, he must've really been great."

Edith quickly wiped her eyes, a gesture unnoticed by her two scavenging grandchildren. "Honey, your grandpa was a great man and for years we made a great team. Now I've got to be strong all by myself. . . ." As Edith's voice trailed off, her thoughts completed the sentence, *and find my bearings again.*

four

"Grandma, this has been the best Christmas ever," Jay exclaimed as he lay on the floor of Edith's living room trying to figure out the rules of his newest computer game.

"Every Christmas is special to me," she assured him. "Especially when I am surrounded by such a loving family. I only wish that Jean and Jim were here to share the holidays with us."

"I like Christmas because Daddy spends the day with us instead of always leaving to go back to the store," Dawn interjected as she hugged her father who was busy reading the *Wall Street Journal*.

To Edith the day had been truly delightful, but that euphoric feeling was short-lived. While Nancy was helping Edith prepare evening sandwiches from ham left over from dinner, the younger woman laid the knife on the counter and sunk into a nearby kitchen chair.

"Mom, this is a hard subject to bring up, but I just have to talk to someone," she confided with tears beginning to build in her eyes. "I know you're Bob's mother, but you've been like a mother to me, especially after my own mother passed away." Nancy paused for a moment and then blurted out, "Do you think it's possible that Bob is being unfaithful to me?"

Edith's felt her hands turn cold and clammy. She seated herself on a nearby chair. "Whatever gave you

39

that idea?"

"Well, nothing specifically, but he's become so distant lately. He seems to be spending every waking hour at the store."

"Have you seen any signs that might suggest another woman?" Edith asked. Nancy shook her head.

"Have you found letters, perhaps lipstick on his clothes, or received any unexplained phone calls?"

Nancy continued to shake her head. "Well, no, but there has to be something going on. We aren't nearly as close as we used to be. When we were first married Bob would tell me every detail of his life and we would spend a lot of time together. We'd take long walks or drive to the country. Now he spends all his time at the store without me."

"Nancy, don't jump to the wrong conclusion," Edith calmly reminded her. "Bob is probably not having an affair with another woman, but rather a love affair with building a successful business."

Edith took her daughter-in-law's hand. "I've noticed the store seems to consume him. It's painful now, but I'm sure with time this too will pass away. Many men go through this as they begin to achieve a certain amount of success in their careers."

"I hope so," Nancy said with a faint smile. "I knew if I talked to you, you'd understand what was happening."

Their conversation was interrupted by the shrill ring of the telephone. Edith hurried to answer it with a "Merry Christmas," as she put the phone to her ear.

It was Jean. "Merry Christmas to you. Are you having a nice holiday?"

After exchanging family news with both Jean and Jim, Edith passed the phone on to Nancy, then Bob, Jay, and Dawn. Each had a chance to share their Christmas greetings. Geographical distance could not dampen their family love.

When the mantel clock struck nine times that night, Bob called an end to the visit. "Time to head home, kids. Gather up your toys. Mom, can I see you in the kitchen for a minute?"

Bob motioned for her to sit while he paced around the room. "Mom, why don't you reconsider going to Sun City this winter? There is nothing for you to do here in Rocky Bluff until spring. I can take over full control of the store, and you won't have a thing to worry about. Maybe you could look up the Millers and begin playing golf again."

Edith took a long deep breath to calm herself before responding. "You're mistaken, Bob. There's plenty for me to do here in Rocky Bluff. Now that the holidays are over I plan to find a part-time job, or I may get involved in volunteer work."

As she surveyed her son's determined eyes and set jaw, she tried to control her anger. "Again I want to remind you that Harkness Hardware is a family business, not a sole proprietorship."

"I'm sure you'll see it my way when the holiday excitement is over," Bob mumbled as he left the kitchen and turned his attention to the children. He helped them gather their packages and put on their coats. He left with only a cool thank you to his mother.

Edith stood in the window and watched them leave with tears in her eyes. She could face retirement, but the conflict with her son was another matter.

The next morning Edith stayed in bed later than usual after a fitful night's sleep. At nine-fifteen she wrapped her fleece robe around her and went to the front door to collect the morning paper from between the storm door and inside door. Unfolding the *Rocky Bluff Herald* she scanned the headlines and lead story.

LOCAL YOUTH DEAD OF OVERDOSE

Susan Youngman, seventeen-year-old daughter of Frank and Elizabeth Youngman, was found dead in her bedroom late Christmas night. Police found an empty bottle of unidentified pills beside her. An autopsy is being performed.

Edith remembered the blond-haired student in her last home economics class. She would have given her an A for the semester if she had a better fit on her final sewing project. Her eyes filled with tears as she stepped back into the warmth of her living room and closed the door and continued reading.

The victim had placed a call to the Rocky Bluff Crisis Center at 9:15 P.M. Because of the holiday season the volunteer force was insufficient to handle the overload of calls and Susan was put on hold. When the volunteer returned to Susan's call there was no answer. The

call was traced to the Youngman residence and police were summoned.

Funeral services will be held at 1:00
P.M. on December 30 at the First Presbyterian Church of Rocky Bluff. Interment
will follow at the Pine Hills Memorial
Cemetery.

I've got to go to those services, Edith determined as
she sank into the rocking chair beside the window.
Reaching for a tissue on the end table beside her, she
sobbed softly as her mind drifted back to the two years
she had Susan as a student.

*Susan had always been a shy girl without many
friends. Was there anything I could have done to help
prevent this tragedy?* Edith reached for another tissue.
Her eyes wandered to the freshly fallen snow outside
the window.

*Could I have helped raise her self-esteem so that
she would not have drifted to this level of hopeless-
ness? Should I have referred her to the counselors when
I noticed her avoiding the other girls?* After spending
a few minutes lost in grief, Edith reached for the telephone.

After hearing her daughter-in-law's voice on the other
end of the line, she said, "Nancy, did you see this
morning's paper?"

"You mean about Susan Youngman? Was she one of
your students?"

"Yes, she was such a sweet girl. Do you think you
could attend the funeral with me Friday?"

"Of course, Mom. We'll get someone to cover for

me at the store. Besides, Susan's parents are regular customers. The least I can do is lend some support during this tragic time."

That Friday the First Presbyterian Church was packed with mourners. One section was exclusively high school students. Afterward as the crowd gathered at the Pine Hills Cemetery, Edith found herself surrounded by teenagers. Not only were her former students anxious to learn about her activities since she'd retired, but they craved her motherly support during their time of grief. Many of them had never lost a loved one. To them death only came to the elderly, not someone their own age, someone who had taken her own life.

The following Monday Edith spotted an advertisement in the classified section of the morning paper.

> WANTED: CRISIS CENTER VOLUNTEERS
> No Experience Necessary
> Training Classes Begin January 10th
> To Preregister Call 789-3333.

That's exactly what I want to do, she thought excitedly. *I can take these classes and then work at the Crisis Center. Maybe I can make a difference for all the other Susan Youngmans who are out there crying for someone to listen to them.*

Edith grabbed the phone and dialed the advertised number. After the second ring a man answered. "Hello, Crisis Center. May I help you?"

"I saw your ad in the paper about training sessions for volunteers. I'm interested in more of the details."

"Good, I'm glad you called," a gentle male voice

replied. "There's a twelve week training session. During that time we determine who is suitable for the task. We're in desperate need of more volunteers. Could you give me your name and tell me a little about yourself and why you would like to help at the Crisis Center?"

"My name is Edith Harkness. I retired from teaching at Rocky Bluff High School last year and I'd like to devote a few hours a week to community service. I had Susan Youngman in my class and I'm willing to do whatever I can to help prevent another such tragedy."

"Mrs. Harkness, thank you for calling. I'm Roy Dutton, the director of the Crisis Center. I'll be leading the sessions and bringing in several specialists as guest lecturers. I'm looking forward to meeting you in person. Can you come to the first training session Monday, January tenth, at seven P.M. in the hospitality room of the Civic Center?"

"Yes, I'll be glad to learn more about it. I'm looking forward to being there."

After they'd hung up Edith paused to enjoy the warm glow that enveloped her. Now she would finally be contributing something to the community that she loved.

The next few days seemed to drag by as Edith sought ways to fill her time. Monday evening the street lights glistened on the freshly fallen snow as Edith drove cautiously down Main Street to the Civic Center. A twinge of doubt haunted her. *At my age why do I think I'll be able to help young people going through problems so different from what I faced as a teenager? Although I've experienced my share of heartaches I've led a fairly protected life compared to the temptations they face today.*

Edith parked her Ford Escort next to the side door of the Civic Center and wrapped her scarf around her face to protect against the harsh Montana wind. She hurried inside and located the meeting room at the end of the hallway. Seated at three tables were ten young women and five men. She was the only woman over thirty.

A distinguished looking gray-haired gentleman whom Edith vaguely recognized from church rose to greet her. "Welcome. You must be Edith Harkness. I'm Roy Dutton. I'm glad the cold weather didn't keep you away. Would you like to hang up your coat and join us?"

As Edith took a seat at the end of the far table, the director walked to the front of the room. "I'd like to welcome all of you to our first in a series of twelve training sessions for Crisis Center volunteers. Would each of you introduce yourself and tell us why you are interested in crisis intervention?"

After the introductions Roy began his presentation by distributing handouts describing the schedule of classes, the topics to be covered, and the guest speakers for the various class sessions. Edith quickly forgot her apprehension as she became engrossed in the techniques used in helping people in crisis. In no time at all Roy Dutton announced that it was nine o'clock and the session had ended.

As Edith was buttoning her coat, Roy approached her. "I'd like to say again how glad I am that you decided to join our group. We have been in dire need of mature people. The twenty year olds may be able to talk the language of those in crisis, but it has been my experience that troubled people have more confidence in older volunteers. Maturity has a way of providing stability and hope in what appears to be an impossible situation."

"I would like to think I have learned a few things during all my years of living, but the problems young people face today are so different from those I faced growing up."

"Yes and no," the director responded kindly. "Yes, young people are faced with problems of drugs, sex, and violence that were not as prevalent a few years ago. However, people still have the same basic needs of love, acceptance, and a feeling that their life has a meaning or purpose. Our biggest job is to strip away all the circumstantial smoke screens and get to the core of the problem. How about joining me across the street at Bea's for a cup of coffee? We can continue our discussion there."

Leaving her car in the parking lot of the Civic Center, Edith walked across the street with Roy. His calm and direct manner put her completely at ease.

After ordering coffee and pie, the conversation shifted from the Crisis Center to their families. Roy was aware of Harkness Hardware but had not made the family connection between Bob Harkness and Edith. After expressing concern about Edith's difficult transition into retirement, he began to share his own background.

"I guess I've lived a humble life compared to owning a hardware store and teaching school. I was a social worker all my life. I have one son, Pete, who absorbed most of my spare time. His was a difficult birth.

The doctor was able to save his life, but he was left with some brain damage from lack of oxygen. Then when he was three years old his mother developed cancer. We lost her a year later."

"I'm sorry to hear that. What a tremendous challenge to raise a handicapped child alone!"

"It was hard at times but I just did what had to be done, the same as anyone would under similar circumstances. There's a terrific special education program here in Rocky Bluff. I don't know what I'd have done without it."

Edith admired his deep blue eyes and practical approach to life as he continued telling her about his son. "Where is Pete now?" she queried. "Still living at home?"

"No, while he was still in school they discovered that he had an unusual mechanical ability and were able to find a job for him as a handyman on a ranch near the Canadian border. He's coming home this weekend. I'd love to have you meet him."

"I'd like that very much."

"How about Friday night? After I meet his bus we have a normal ritual of going to McDonald's."

"Sounds like fun," Edith said genuinely.

"Good, I'll pick you up at five-thirty so you can come to the bus station with me." Roy reached for the check the waitress had left on the table. "I hope you don't mind fast food?"

"Of course not. I frequently end up at those places with my grandchildren."

That Friday evening Roy and Edith waited in the Rocky Bluff bus terminal for the familiar Mountain

Trailways bus to arrive. At exactly five-forty-five headlights shone through the windows as the sixty-passenger bus pulled to a stop. Pete was the first one to step from the bus.

"Hello, Dad," he shouted as he hurried toward his father. "Can we go to McDonald's now? I'm hungry."

"Welcome home, Pete. As soon as we get your bags we can be off, but first I'd like you to meet a friend of mine, Edith Harkness."

Pete stared at the attractive, dark-haired woman standing next to his father. A look of bewilderment crossed his face. "Hello," he mumbled. "Me and my dad are going to McDonald's now."

"Hello, Pete. I'm glad to meet you," Edith said. "I've heard so many good things about you."

Roy tried to diffuse the awkward situation. "Pete, I've invited Edith to join us for hamburgers."

Pete remained silent as Roy took his baggage check and went to claim Pete's worn brown suitcase. Roy then led the way across the snow-packed parking lot to his aging Oldsmobile. He opened the back door of the car and Pete grudgingly slid onto the seat as Roy opened the front door for Edith.

Edith and Roy engaged in small talk as Pete sat glumly in the back. Upon arriving at McDonald's Pete rushed to the counter.

"I'll have two Big Macs, a large order of fries, and a large chocolate milkshake," he told the counter employee as she quietly pushed the order buttons in front of her. After Roy and Edith had placed their order, Roy paid the bill and picked up the tray and followed Pete to a back booth.

"Why'd she have to come?" Pete demanded as he reached for his hamburger. "It's always been just you and me. That's the way it's supposed to be."

Edith shot an uncomfortable glance at Roy.

"Pete, it's always nice to make new friends. Edith is my friend and she wants to be your friend too."

"No, she doesn't," Pete responded sharply. "She only wants to be *your* friend. I watched the way you acted in the car. You didn't even care if I was there or not."

Edith sat quietly as Roy tried to explain their budding friendship to Pete. Roy had been the center of Pete's life for so long that Pete was unable to accept the fact that his father could have a relationship with anyone else. To Pete, Edith was simply a rival for his father's affection. Friendship appeared out of the question, for now.

five

"All of you know it's been a long, cold winter in central Montana," Roy Dutton said at the beginning of the fifth training session. "Cabin fever has settled over Rocky Bluff and calls to the Crisis Center have doubled."

Of the original fifteen volunteers only five had continued the training program: Two were young housewives, one a bus driver, one a high school history teacher, and Edith.

"Because of the increased demand for more counselors I would like all of you to complete the training as soon as possible. How many of you could come four nights a week for the next two weeks?" Roy looked from student to student.

The participants exchanged questioning glances. Finally Edith broke the silence. "I'm free for the next two weeks."

One by one the others echoed their agreement.

Roy smiled with appreciation. "Fine, then, we'll go ahead and meet since most of you are able to be here. If something comes up and you can't come, maybe you could get the notes from someone else. Better yet, I can tape each session."

The next two weeks flew by as Edith spent every Monday through Thursday night in class. Edith's family, however, was less than ecstatic about her involvement. Nancy and Jean were pleased she'd finally found fulfillment. Jay and Dawn continued to spend part of each Saturday with their grandmother and weren't even aware of her other interest. Bob felt the Crisis Center was complete foolishness, but he was glad that his mother's attention had shifted from store affairs.

At every training session Roy presented mock situations of different types of crisis calls. The trainees answered as if each call were a true-to-life one and they had to produce immediate verbal responses. Afterward everyone criticized the simulated crises. This became the most vital part of their training. Besides the guest lecturers from the welfare office and police department, a psychologist from the mental health clinic and a medical doctor offered helpful advice, but they in reality could only supplement the crisis intervention practice. The Crisis Center was only as effective as its volunteers' responses.

Finally the last night arrived and each trainee was handed a certificate of achievement. As Edith examined hers, she felt a satisfaction that rivaled that of receiving her college diploma many years before. Her most recent educational experience, however, had imparted an immeasurable benefit: She had learned more about helping others help themselves than during her four years in undergraduate school.

Following the last class session Roy and Edith shared their customary cup of coffee at Bea's. "Edith, I don't have enough people to fill the schedule at the center this weekend. Would you mind helping Friday and Saturday nights until midnight? We're the busiest over the weekends and occasionally I have two lines going at the same time. I'll be there to help, but after a few calls I'm sure you'll feel confident enough to handle them on your own."

"Sounds good to me. I should try while it's fresh in my mind."

"Good. I'll pick you up at seven-forty-five Friday. If you'd like, bring something to help you pass the time. Some nights the phone rings constantly and other times I can sit for hours and nothing happens, except that I get a lot of reading done."

Friday night Roy arrived as planned and shook the snow from his boots before stepping inside. "Mabel will be there until we arrive," he informed Edith. "Most of the calls come after nine. The desperate ones seem to phone after the movie is over and people return to their empty homes."

On the way to the Crisis Center Roy explained the personal situations of those who had been calling regularly. "None of the regular calls during the last few few months was life-threatening situations, just lonely people. But you never know, there are several delicate relationships that could erupt anytime."

As Roy parked his car in front of the center Edith turned to him. "Thanks for the advice. I can use all the help I can get."

The pair hurried inside to escape the bitter cold and hung their coats on a rack behind the door. Across the room were two newly constructed desk cubicles with phones, paper and pencils, and a list of phone numbers of service agencies. Roy carefully reviewed which buttons to push for each line and which one to use to keep the call on hold and how to notify the telephone company to trace a call.

After Edith felt confident with the use of the phone, they made themselves comfortable on the fading green sofa that had been donated by one of the city council members. They were soon involved in a lively conversation that jumped from world affairs to their families. Just as Roy had said, the phone did not ring for almost two hours. While Edith talked, she crocheted several inches on her afghan and nearly forgot her reason for being there.

At nine-fifty-seven the shrill ringing of the telephone brought them both to attention.

"You're on," Roy whispered as Edith reached for the phone.

"Hello, Crisis Center. How may I help you?"

"I don't know if anyone can help." The man's voice was slurred and he spoke slowly and deliberately.

"Would you like me to try?" Edith asked, giving Roy a desperate glance.

"Well . . . it's kind of personal. My wife just took our baby daughter and left me. I don't know where they went. I called her mother's house but she wasn't there."

Edith gave Roy another panicky look before she answered. "Do you have any idea why she left?"

"Well . . . it's sort of a long story," he mumbled. "I was coming out of Tony's Place as the movie was getting out. I stood there watching the people when I saw Sarah come out with another guy."

His voice broke while Edith waited patiently for him to regain his composure. "I followed them to the parking lot behind the theater. When I confronted them this creep took a swing and leveled me."

"Were you hurt?" Edith's voice displayed her concern.

"No . . . I laid there for a moment, but I was okay. When I finally got home Sarah was just walking out the door with a suitcase in one hand and our baby in the other. Over her shoulder she shouted, 'Don't call me, I'll call you.'"

"What did you do then?"

"I was going to run after her but there was a black sedan with the same fellow in it waiting across the street. He shook his fist at me as she jumped into the car and they sped around the corner. They could be clear to Billings by now."

"That must've really hurt when she left without an explanation." Edith took a deep breath. "I am concerned about you. Have you been able to think about what you should do next?"

"I'm furious with the guy who took my wife. I would blow him away if I had half a chance. I don't understand how Sarah could do this to me. I love her so much. There isn't anything I wouldn't do for her. We have the sweetest six-month-old baby who's the spittin' image of her mother. My entire life centers around them. Without them there's no reason for me to go on living."

Cold chills went through Edith as she listened to his anger. She was reminded of Larry Reynolds. "Do you have any friends?"

"Well, there's a couple . . . but they're happily married. They'd never understand how Sarah could run off with another man. They think the world of her and probably would think I did something to drive her away. Besides, I wouldn't want to bother them with my troubles." His sad voice faltered as he shared his broken heart.

"Friends are for the bad times as well as the good," Edith tried to assure him. "I'm your friend and I'm concerned about your problems. My name is Edith. You don't have to give me your name, but what can I call you over the phone?"

"Jake . . . Jake Croder."

Edith listened to Jake pour out a lifetime of hurts and heartaches. After forty minutes she was able to convince him to make an appointment with one of the counselors at the local mental health center the next morning. She promised to call him the next day to see how he was doing. Fortunately another call did not come in during that time so Roy was able to give his undivided attention to monitoring Jake's call.

"Good work," Roy praised as she hung up the phone with a sigh of relief. "I couldn't have done a better job myself."

"Thanks," Edith mumbled, laying her head on the desk to relax. "That was harder work than I expected. I certainly hope he keeps his word and sees one of the counselors tomorrow. If his wife doesn't come back it will be a long time before he recovers."

Saturday night was even busier for Edith. Most of the callers needed someone to listen to their problems and could then find a solution themselves. In spite of the numerous calls there were long periods of time when neither line was busy and Roy and Edith engaged in personal conversation.

When the next shift of volunteers came at midnight, the older couple put on their coats and walked toward Roy's car parked in the back lot. "Can I pick you up for church in the morning? Pete is home again this weekend and will be with me. I could stop about ten-fifteen and we could make it a threesome."

"I'd love to." After a long pause she giggled. "We'll be the talk of the town by Monday morning."

Hurrying up her front steps Edith turned on the light in the living room and hung her coat in the front closet. She stretched out in her recliner to relax before going to bed. A warm feeling enveloped her as she thought about her friendship with Roy. The warmth quickly faded as she considered Pete's hostility toward her.

I wonder how Pete will react toward me tomorrow at church when he wouldn't even speak to me at McDonald's the other night. I'll have to try my hardest to win him over. I wonder if Roy is actually aware of the depth of Pete's hostility.

When Roy stopped the car in front of Edith's home the next morning, Pete mechanically got into the back seat without saying a word. He continued to sulk as the two in the front seat carried on a lively conversation. The happier they appeared, the more miserable Pete became.

"Pete, how was work on the farm?" Edith asked, trying to pull him into the conversation.

"Okay," he mumbled.

"Did you have a good bus ride?" she probed.

"Nope."

Edith turned her attention back to Roy as he pulled into the church parking lot. Roy opened the car door for Edith as Pete bounded out of the back seat. In the church they found vacant seats in the third pew from the back and waited in silence for the service to begin. Edith felt as if all eyes were on Roy and her. She chuckled to herself as she imagined what they might be thinking.

Pete's scowl continued during the entire service; any gestures of kindness to share a hymnal were quickly rebuffed. When the service was over Pete hurried to the door, while Roy and Edith tried to keep up with him and still greet those around them.

"Good morning, Mrs. Harkness." Pastor Rhodes smiled as he vigorously shook her hand. "How are you today?"

"Very well, thank you," she answered graciously as the minister turned to greet Roy.

"I see your son is home," Pastor Rhodes said as he shook Roy's hand. "It must be a special treat to have him with you."

"Dad hasn't any time for me," Pete interrupted rudely. "He's been too busy with Edith."

Pastor Rhodes gulped, his face flushed. "Your dad loves you just as much as he always has. I'm sure you will enjoy getting to know Mrs. Harkness. She's an excellent teacher and has a special love for young people."

"She doesn't love me," Pete blurted out as he shoved his way through the crowd into the parking lot.

"Please excuse his outburst," Roy apologized. "He usually loves everyone, but he's had a hard time accepting Edith's friendship."

"I understand. Think nothing of it. Maybe I'll be

able to talk with Pete sometime this week."

"That would be thoughtful of you, but the Davidsons are picking him up this afternoon and taking him back to the ranch," Roy explained as the minister turned his attention to greeting the next person in line.

Following a quick lunch, and without saying another word to his father, Pete hurried into his bedroom and began repacking his clothes. Normally he would have waited for his father's help but today was different. As soon as the familiar gold Jeep Wagoneer stopped in front of the Dutton home, Pete bounded for the car without even a goodbye.

The following afternoon as Roy sat in his easy chair reading the current issue of *U.S. News and World Report*, the doorbell rang. He opened the door to his minister. "Pastor Rhodes, what a pleasant surprise. Do come in. Let me take your coat."

"When Pete left church yesterday I was extremely concerned about him." The minister made himself comfortable on the living room sofa.

"Pastor Rhodes, I've never seen him this upset before. I thought he would take kindly to Edith but he's acting like a spoiled child."

"Mentally and emotionally Pete will always be a child. I hope you don't dampen your friendship with Edith because of it. You can't let Pete think he has control over you or he'll take advantage of the situation."

"But what can I do? I've tried everything I can think of and it only gets worse," Roy admitted, hoping for even a thread of insight into his dilemma.

"Maybe a few days away from home with your

undivided attention would help. Would it be possible to take Pete on an extended fishing trip later in the spring? He used to enjoy your trips to Colorado."

"That's an excellent idea. Maybe then he'll realize that I'll always love him despite my friendship with Edith."

"Does Pete remember his mother at all?" Pastor Rhodes inquired as he thought back through the years of his relationship with the father and son.

"Not really. He's seen a lot of pictures of her though." He paused a moment and stared blankly out the window at the thawing snow. "Come to think of it, he's never had a good relationship with any woman. When he was in school he usually had male teachers so perhaps he doesn't know how to interact with a mother substitute."

"That could be possible."

"He's accepted Martha Davidson, but their relationship is a more distant employer-employee arrangement. Martha's temperament displays her German background: hard-working, reserved, rarely displaying her true feelings." Roy tried to analyze his son's behavior. "I guess I'll just have to keep working on the situation and see what happens. It couldn't possibly get any worse than it already is."

"Let me know if there's anything I can do," Pastor Rhodes offered as he stood up to leave. "If you'd like, I'd be glad to meet with Pete when he comes home next time."

"Thanks for your concern," Roy said, walking him to the door. "I'll definitely be in touch."

Returning to his favorite chair Roy sat bewildered.

What should I do about Pete? He's the last person on earth I'd want to hurt, but he refuses to accept Edith . . . Maybe that fishing trip would be a good idea. Perhaps while we're alone in the Colorado wilderness I can make him understand my need for female companionship. . . Maybe it wasn't wise for me to have devoted so much time to Pete when he was growing up while ignoring my own needs. I should have known that sooner or later I would become interested in another woman.

The next Sunday afternoon Edith enjoyed the day with her family. Bob was absorbed with the figures on his laptop computer. Nancy worked on a pile of mending while she visited with her mother-in-law. As soon as possible the children monopolized Edith's time with table games. After an hour and a half Edith's desire flagged while the children were still going strong.

As the children finished gathering up the game pieces, Nancy joined her mother-in-law at the card table in the center of the living room. "Mom, can I get you a cup of coffee?"

"After a game like that I think I deserve one along with some adult companionship," Edith answered light-heartedly.

As Nancy prepared the coffee, Edith joined her son on the sofa. "Bob, you've been so quiet this afternoon. Is something on your mind?"

Bob shifted positions and cleared his throat. "Actually, Mom, I've been wanting to talk to you for some time but I didn't know how or when."

"Just go ahead and say it and maybe together we can

put it in the proper words."

Nancy returned with the coffee for her mother-in-law and a refill for her husband and herself. "Is this a private conversation or can anybody join?"

"Don't be silly," Bob answered, ignoring her dry humor. "This is a family affair. Maybe you could help explain this to Mother."

"Explain what?"

"Well, w-what exactly is your relationship with Roy Dutton?" Bob stammered, avoiding his mother's annoyed gaze.

"We are becoming very close friends. I help him at least twice a week at the Crisis Center, but you know all that. Why do you ask?"

"Can't you see what he's trying to do?" Bob demanded in a condescending tone.

"He's trying to help those in the community who are going through a difficult period in their lives. What's wrong with that?" Edith didn't try to hide the irritation in her voice.

"Is Roy showing a romantic interest in you?" Bob boldly continued.

Edith felt her cheeks redden. "We're becoming fond of each other and we're discovering that we share many of the same interests and hobbies. So again I ask, what's wrong with that?"

"He's taking advantage of your situation, Mom. Can't you see? You've just retired and don't know what direction you should take and a gray-haired knight in shining armor comes along and tries to sweep you off your feet."

Edith's eyes danced with anger. "Bob, that isn't

exactly the way it happened. We began by having coffee together after classes, a normal situation, wouldn't you say? Then a friendship developed."

"Let's approach it from a different angle. What kind of work did Roy do before he retired?"

"I've told you that he was a social worker."

"And what kind of income do retired social workers have?"

"I really haven't given it much thought. I assume he receives social security and a stipend from the Montana Public Employees Retirement Fund. He doesn't seem to have any overwhelming financial need, nor is he living extravagantly."

"But Mother, can't you see what he's interested in? It's a classic soap opera. I can't stand by and let a Prince Charming who is barely making an existence sweet talk you out of all your savings. The money my father made belongs in the family, not to a fast-talking, gray-haired panther."

"Bob, that is the most absurd thing I have ever heard! Where does it say that every man over sixty-five who takes a woman to coffee is interested only in her money? We have the same need for human companionship as those under thirty."

As the tension mounted in the Harkness living room, Nancy again found herself in the position of family mediator. "I'm sure Bob doesn't mean to sound so cruel," she said as she shot a warning look at Bob. "If he knew Roy the way you do, I know he'd feel differently about the situation. Let's change the subject to something more pleasant. We invited you over to have an enjoyable afternoon, not to condemn your friendship."

"Thanks, Nancy. Where is the skirt you want me to hem? If you'll slip it on I'll measure and pin it up for you."

For the next couple of hours Edith and Nancy worked in the bedroom that doubled as a sewing room. No mention of Bob's outburst was made, but his words had left a scar that would be hard to heal. Edith's thoughts, however, raged just beneath her calm exterior. If only her son would try to understand life from her point of view.

six

"Hello, Mom," Jean said as Edith answered the phone late one Friday night in April. "I hope I didn't wake you. How's the weather in Montana?"

"Hi, dear. I'd just dozed off. It's good to hear your voice," Edith responded, waking from a light sleep. "To answer your important question, I hope spring has finally come. The snow is gone except on the mountain peaks and I have a couple tulips trying to force their way through the ground."

"Good. I hope you don't have any late spring blizzards this year. They are the real killers. At least the weather isn't nearly as severe here in Chamberland."

"Jean, what's up? You didn't call me at ten-thirty to talk about the weather."

"I called at ten-thirty because the rates are cheaper, and to give you some good news."

"Don't keep me in suspense."

"You're going to have another grandchild."

Edith was now wide awake. "I'm so happy for you, Jean. When's the baby due?"

"The doctor says the middle of October. I hope that I'll be able to keep working through August. Jim's so excited about the baby that he has already become overly protective of me. I keep trying to convince him that pregnancy is a natural, normal condition, but he's carrying on as if our baby will be the first one born in history."

"Keep me posted on how you are getting along. Tell me if there is anything I can do to help."

"You don't have to worry about anything, Mother. I haven't been a nurse for six years for nothing. Sorry I woke you. I'd better let you go so you can get some sleep. Good night, Mom."

"Good night, dear. Take care of yourself and that new grandbaby."

As Edith drifted off to sleep that night, a sense of peace filled her. She was proud of her family and their accomplishments; she felt blessed to have Roy with whom she could share the joys and frustrations of life. She'd have to tell him the exciting news first thing in the morning.

Pete's emotions were in constant confusion. When he returned to the ranch after his two-week visit in Rocky Bluff, he kept busy with farm chores. In the evenings he hid himself in his room and put model engines together. He didn't speak about his father for several days. One afternoon when he returned to the farmhouse after helping with the calves, Martha met him at the door.

"Pete, your dad called this afternoon."

"I never want to talk to him again," Pete said, pouting and stomping his foot in disgust. "He loves Edith, not me."

"But Pete, he called specifically to talk to you, but you were out haying the new calves and I couldn't find you in time. Why don't you call him back?"

"I won't do it."

"Your dad mentioned something about taking you on a fishing trip to Colorado. Why would you turn down a trip like that? I always thought you liked to fish."

Pete looked at Martha Davidson in disbelief. Gradually the tension left his face. "Well . . . maybe I'll call him. Can I have time off work to go on a trip?"

Martha breathed a sigh of relief. "Certainly. Now why don't you give your father a call and see what he has planned?"

Martha handed a reluctant Pete the telephone and slowly he dialed his father's number.

"Hello, Dutton residence."

"Hi, Dad. Martha said I should call you."

"I'm glad you did, Pete. How have you been?"

"I'm fine. Martha said you're going fishing in Colorado."

"Yes, and I was wondering if you would like to come with me."

Pete paused, torn between going on the fishing trip and avoiding Edith. "I'll go only if it's just you and me."

"I assure you it'll just be the two of us. I've already made the reservations at the Blue Lodge on Lake Branby for the twenty-first to the twenty-seventh of April. We should have a lot of fun. They say that April is the best time to catch rainbow trout and walleye."

"Okay. I'll go with you."

"Have all your things ready on the twenty-first and we'll leave bright and early. Mrs. Davidson invited me to spend the night with you at the ranch so we can get an early start. It's a long day's drive for us."

"I'll be ready. Thanks, Dad." With the promise of a week alone with his dad, Pete was back to his normal, talkative self. *Maybe I'll be able to convince Dad to forget all about his lady friend,* he thought eagerly.

Roy hung up the phone with a feeling of triumph. Pastor Rhodes must have been right. A fishing trip alone with Pete is a great idea. He poured a glass of milk and cut himself a large piece of chocolate cake. After enjoying his snack he called Edith to share the progress he was making with Pete. At last he had found someone who understood some of the problems of raising a handicapped child.

Three weeks later Roy and Pete left Montana as scheduled. After crossing the Colorado border on Interstate 25, the car began to lose power. Each hill became harder and harder to climb.

"Dad," Pete began with a worried look on his face, "would you turn off the radio? I want to listen to the engine. I think I know what's wrong."

Roy immediately turned off the radio and they both listened intently as the car slowly reached the crest of another hill. "What do you think it is, son?" Long ago Roy had learned that although his son was classified as mentally retarded, he was a near genius when it came to mechanical things.

"I think the timing is off. Would you stop so I can check it?"

Ten miles farther down the road Roy pulled the loaded car into a shaded rest area. Pete jumped out and opened the hood. His eyes lit up. "Dad, do you have a screwdriver? The timing is off. All it needs is a little adjusting."

Roy reached into the glove compartment and handed the tool to his son.

Moments later the engine was purring like a kitten. "There," Pete said with obvious pride. "The car should run all right now."

The two men climbed back into the car and within minutes they were cruising up a steep incline at sixty-five miles an hour without a problem. They made the rest of the trip without incident and at seven that evening Pete caught sight of Lake Branby. "Dad, look at the lake! It's beautiful. I can hardly wait to get out on the water."

The pair quickly unloaded the car and began preparing hot dogs and beans on the cabin hotplate. The lumpy beds supplied relief for their tired bodies. At dawn Roy and Pete were on the lake. The wind was biting and cold as it blew off the water but they were both bundled in warm clothing and enjoyed the invigorating air. Little time passed before Roy pulled in a three-pound rainbow trout and a half-hour later Pete caught a walleye.

As the morning warmed, Pete shed one of his jackets. "Dad, do you love Edith?" he asked unexpectedly.

Roy paused. He had been wondering how he could bring up the subject but this wasn't the way he'd anticipated. "Yes, I'm very fond of her."

"Are you going to marry her?"

"We don't have any definite plans," Roy replied hesitantly.

"Men always marry their girlfriends. I've seen it all on TV."

"Why are you worrying about me getting married?"

"Because then you won't have any time for me. You'll only have time for your wife."

Again Roy tried to explain that there would always be enough love to go around. Pete didn't respond but continued to stare blankly at the horizon.

For the remainder of the week their relationship was strained. Pete responded only to direct questions. His mood was cold and he displayed no emotion. Pete's mind was made up. If his father got married he would lose him forever.

Roy was more concerned how he could communicate with Pete. Even a long-distance phone call to Edith gave him no new ideas.

The last afternoon on the lake Roy tried again to help his son understand the situation. "Pete, you've been the center of my life for the last twenty-eight years and I love you dearly," he began cautiously. "But ever since your mother died there has been an empty spot in my life, that is, until I met Edith. But Edith will never change our relationship."

"I don't want to talk about Edith. You love her more than you love me. I want to go back to the ranch."

"The Davidsons will be coming to Rocky Bluff three days after we get back. That way you'll have time to see your old friends before going back to work and we can have a little more time together."

The long fishing vacation had ended on a sour note. Neither father nor son had accomplished his secret objective. The drive back to Montana was uneventful. Pete slept most of the way or stared blankly at the scenery. His normal zest for life seemed to have vanished.

Roy's confusion about how to handle his son's jealousy increased with each passing mile. I'm able to help others deal with their problems, but I'm not able to deal with my own, he scolded himself as he followed his son into their home late that night.

Roy skipped church the next morning and unpacked the car. Pete continued to pout and avoid his father. He only left the TV to go to the kitchen or to the bathroom. Any offer of warmth by his father was rebuffed.

Monday morning Pete became even more bored and decided to take a walk around his hometown to enjoy the fresh spring air. As he stopped to look into each of the store windows, one particular store caught his attention: Harkness Hardware. Pete opened the double doors and quietly strolled down a side aisle. He began to idly examine the car repair tools. Within a few minutes a handsome, dark-haired man approached. "May I help you?"

"No, I'm just browsing," Pete mumbled.

"Say, aren't you Roy Dutton's son?"

"Yes. My name is Pete. What's yours?" He looked up from the display of sockets.

"I'm Bob Harkness. I imagine you know my mother, Edith."

Pete's body tensed. "I wish your mother would stay away from my dad. I don't like her."

"Pete, you must really be upset about their relationship. Let's go across the street to the drugstore and have a cup of coffee and talk about it. My wife Nancy can watch the store while I'm gone."

Pete felt important in the company of such an influential businessperson. He and his father had often had coffee accompanied by someone whom Pete felt was important, but never had anyone like that invited him for coffee. Pete obediently followed Bob into the drugstore. The two men found a back booth and ordered.

As the waitress returned with two steaming cups, Bob looked intently at Pete. "Why are you so upset about our parents' relationship?"

"My dad doesn't need a wife," Pete protested adamantly. "He only needs a son."

"Do you suppose he's just looking for a woman to do his housekeeping for him?" Bob asked, hoping to take full advantage of Pete's simple, naive mind.

"Why else do men get married?" Pete asked innocently. After a short time he gave a hearty laugh and answered his own question. "Unless they find someone with a lot of money. I once saw a movie on TV about how this younger man married an old lady only for her money. Does your mother have a lot of money?"

Bob's muscles tightened as he tried to maintain a relaxed smile on his face. "I'm afraid your dad is looking at the wrong woman if he is only looking for money. Is it getting hard for him to live on his pension?"

"I don't know," Pete responded blankly. "He complains a lot about not having much money. Maybe it's because he's spending all his money on your mother. Why don't you stop them?"

"I wish I could but I can't find a way to do it. They're both acting like a couple of silly teenagers instead of mature senior citizens. What would they do if one of them became seriously ill?"

"If my dad got sick I could take care of him myself," Pete boasted as he took his last sip of coffee.

A familiar voice interrupted their conversation. "Is this a private party or can anybody join?"

"Oh, hi, Mom," Bob responded, startled at Edith's sudden appearance. "Please sit down and join us. I was just getting better acquainted with Roy's son."

"Hello, Pete. How was your fishing trip?"

"Fine," he mumbled without looking from his empty coffee cup.

"Did you catch your limit?" Edith continued, hoping to somehow break the ice.

"Of course. I'm a good fisherman."

"When are you going back to the ranch?" Edith persisted, trying every possible way to draw him into a conversation.

"Wednesday. Then you can have my dad all to yourself."

"Pete, your father loves you very much. He talks about you constantly while you're gone."

"I better go now." Without further explanation, Pete rose and hurried from the drugstore.

"I don't know how Roy and I are going to be able to convince Pete that we both love him and want to have him around," Edith sighed to her son.

"Maybe it would be better if you didn't try so hard. It's not fair that you come between a father and son during this stage of their lives." Bob glanced at his wrist-watch. "If you'll excuse me I'd better get back to the store and help Nancy. I've been gone quite a while now and we have a lot of new stock to check in."

The next day Bob dialed the Dutton home. "Hi, Pete. This is Bob. I'm sorry that you're leaving tomorrow to go back to the ranch. The next time you're home would you come to the store and see me? Maybe if we work together we can convince our parents how foolish they are."

"I've tried to break them up and it hasn't worked," Pete answered excitedly. Finally he had met someone who understood his problem. "Dad should be spending more time with me."

"You're right, Pete," Bob continued, trying to incite Pete into action. "They don't belong together. He needs to be spending that time with you." Bob paused for emphasis. "After all, you're his only son."

seven

"Do you have plans for Friday night?" Roy asked after Edith answered her telephone on the last Tuesday in April.

She smiled to herself. "Not really, just the usual 'Friday Night at the Movies' on TV or a good book. Do you have something better in mind?"

"You decide. There's a three-act play at the Civic Center presented by a traveling team of college students. People say they are pretty good. Would you care to join me?"

She chuckled. "What time does it start?"

"It begins at eight, so I'll pick you up about seven-thirty. I'm looking forward to seeing you then," Roy added as he bid her goodbye.

As Roy drove through the brightly lit streets of Rocky Bluff on Friday night, Edith turned to him, her face flushed and palms sweaty. "I almost called and broke our date this evening," she murmured. "I've been feeling very strange most of the day. Probably some kind of virus coming on, what with the chest pains I've had. I figured that I'd feel the same whether I sat home in my easy chair or if I went to the play, so I decided to go ahead and enjoy the play."

"Are you sure you'll be okay?" Roy questioned gently, his blue eyes settling on Edith's tension-filled face. "The rest might be better for you."

"No, I'll be fine, really," Edith assured him as Roy pulled to a stop in the far corner of the Civic Center parking lot.

When they arrived in the lobby they were surprised to find that the main floor of the auditorium was full and only a few seats were left in the balcony. Amid the constant stirring of people, Roy and Edith found two vacant seats close to the aisle near the back of the balcony. After they greeted friends from the senior citizens center in front of them and a couple of Edith's former students nearby, they settled into a few moments of idle chit-chat before the curtain went up.

As the play progressed Edith broke into a cold sweat. Her last conscious thoughts were of Roy. *I shouldn't have come but I don't want to spoil Roy's evening and have him take me home. He has been looking forward to seeing this play all week.*

As the curtain fell after the second act the pain in Edith's chest became unbearable, then she experienced the same horrible sensation traveling down her left arm. With a heavy gasp for air she slumped sideways toward Roy.

"Someone call an ambulance!" he shouted as he stretched Edith out in the aisle. Quickly he checked for a pulse in the carotid artery. Nothing. Tilting her head backward, he cleared Edith's airways and began CPR. Fifteen chest compressions, then two breaths into her mouth, fifteen more chest compressions and two long breaths. After what seemed an eternity Roy heard the sound of an ambulance in the street below. Moments later three emergency medical technicians rushed in with a stretcher.

The ambulance crew quickly assessed the situation and continued CPR as they placed Edith carefully on the stretcher and carried her to the waiting ambulance. Roy hurried to his car and followed them at full speed. His only thought was to get Edith to the hospital immediately.

As Roy entered the emergency room, three minutes behind the ambulance, he was faced with a smiling ambulance crew. "We made it," the short dark-haired attendant shouted as soon as he saw Roy. "She started breathing on her own as we pulled into the hospital parking lot. Thanks to your quick action at the Civic Center, I think we have a good chance of winning this one."

Roy hurried to the admissions desk. "May I see Edith Harkness, please? She just arrived by ambulance."

"I'm sorry, but the doctors are with her now. Are you a member of the family?" The gray-haired nurse behind the desk took out a sheet to record Edith's background data.

"I'm a good friend," Roy replied nervously. "But I'll call them right away. Her son lives here in Rocky Bluff and her daughter is in Idaho."

"I'd appreciate if you'd do that for us. I'll wait for her son to arrive to get her background."

Roy hurried to the nearby phone booth, checked the number, and dialed the Robert Harkness residence. After several rings Jay answered the phone.

"Hello, Jay. Is your daddy home?"

"Just a moment and I'll call him."

A deep voice greeted him after a few moments of silence.

"Hello, Bob. This is Roy Dutton. Your mother and I went to the community play tonight where she became seriously ill. They brought her to the hospital in the ambulance. Would you come right away?"

There was an icy pause at the other end of the line. "I'll be right there. Thanks for calling."

Within ten minutes Bob and Nancy rushed into the emergency room waiting area. "How is she?" Bob demanded as soon as he saw Roy.

"The doctor is waiting to talk to you. Do you mind if I tag along?"

"No, of course not. You might be able to help us fill in the pieces."

Bob stepped up to the admissions clerk. "Could I see Edith Harkness's doctor? I'm her son, Bob."

"Just a moment, please. I'll have to page him."

"Dr. Brewer . . . paging Dr. Brewer . . . please come to the emergency room admissions desk."

Within moments a sandy-haired doctor in a white coat with a stethoscope around his neck appeared. He approached the worried trio. "Are you relatives of Mrs. Harkness?"

"Yes, I'm her son, Bob Harkness, and this is my wife, Nancy, and a friend of my mother's, Roy Dutton."

"It's nice meeting you. Let's sit over here." He motioned to a sofa and loveseat in a corner. They sat on the edge of their seats as the doctor continued. "Your mother is beginning to stabilize, but it will be several days before we know how much damage has been done. I've had her moved into the intensive care unit where we can monitor her heart. We may decide to transport her to the Great Falls Deaconess Hospital where they specialize in cardiac care."

"Is there anything we can do for her?" Nancy asked tearfully.

"Just pray. The medical profession will give her the best care possible, but only God can heal. You might want to call the rest of the family and warn them that she is in critical condition."

"We were planning to call her daughter in Idaho as soon as we'd talked with you and had more details," Roy explained. "I'm sure she'll want to come and be with her."

"I'll be on call all night if your mother needs me," Dr. Brewer assured them. "If you want to go to the ICU unit in the south wing you can see your mother for just a few minutes. She's not fully conscious, but she's beginning to respond to outside stimuli. There's a five-minute visiting limitation per hour. Feel free to call me if you have any questions." With that the physician disappeared down the long corridor to the doctors' lounge while the others sat in stunned silence.

"Let's go see Mother. I'll call Jean later," Bob directed as they rose from their seats at the same time and made their way to the south wing.

After finding the nurse on duty Bob discovered Edith was in room 317. They all peered in through the glass window. "Your mother is resting well, but she's in critical condition. Only one person is allowed in the room at a time," the nurse directed.

Nancy slipped in first. After a few brief moments of watching Edith struggle with each breath, she left the room with tears in her eyes. Roy and Bob took a few moments with her without saying a word. Each was lost in his own thoughts.

As Bob joined the others in the hallway he cleared his throat in an attempt to collect his composure. "I'll give Jean a call if you want to go home and get some rest. There is nothing we can do here. Mom seems to be receiving the best of care."

While Bob made his way to the phone booth next to the hospital lobby, Roy waved a sad farewell and stepped outside. A warm breeze struck his face. Normally he embraced the coming of spring, but tonight his body felt numb. He knew that he was becoming extremely fond of Edith, but he didn't realize how much she meant to him until he saw her lying pale and nearly lifeless in the intensive care unit. The memories of the happy times they had together and the joys they had shared flashed before him.

When he arrived home, Roy fixed himself a cup of hot cocoa and tried to relax. His mind kept drifting back to the hospital. He finally decided to go to bed, but the hours passed slowly as he tossed and turned.

By nine the next morning Roy had returned to the south wing of the hospital. As he approached the nursing station he found Nancy, Bob, and Dr. Brewer in the visitors' lounge. Roy hesitated in the doorway until Bob acknowledged him with a weary smile. "Roy, would you join us? We have some important decisions to make."

Roy took a seat on the couch next to the doctor. "How's Edith this morning?"

"She rested well all night and is beginning to regain consciousness, but she's in a great deal of pain," Dr. Brewer explained. "Bob and I feel it would be wise to transfer her to the Great Falls Deaconness Hospital as soon as possible. The Mercy Flight Ambulance has already been summoned."

"The problem is," Bob began hesitantly, "it will take me most of the day to arrange for help at the store so I can go to Great Falls. I talked with Jean last night and Jim is taking her into Coeur D'Alene this afternoon so that she can catch the evening flight to Great Falls. We need to have someone there to meet her flight at eleven-thirty. Would you be willing to drive to Great Falls and be with Mother and then meet Jean's flight?"

This was one of the most difficult situations Bob had ever faced. He had been trying his best to discourage Roy's friendship with his mother, but now he felt forced into seeking his help. *Maybe if he sees her at her worst it will convince him to end their relationship,* he thought. *Perhaps when he sees all her medical costs he'll really lose interest.*

"Certainly," Roy responded, completely ignorant of Bob's feelings toward him. "I'll go home and pack a few things and leave right away. What time will the air ambulance get into Great Falls?"

"It should be arriving here in about fifteen minutes," Dr. Brewer explained. "It will take less than three minutes to load the patient and then another forty-five minutes to fly back to Deaconess. If you leave right away you might be a little over an hour behind her arrival. I'll let them know that you are coming."

"They're planning to do a heart catheterization soon after she arrives and from there they will decide if open heart surgery is necessary," Bob continued, trying to mask his agitation. "I'll be there first thing tomorrow morning if they do surgery, but it's impossible for me to walk away from the store without prior arrangements."

"There's no problem," Roy assured him. "That's one of the advantages of retirement. I'm free to help anyone at a moment's notice. May I see Edith before I leave?"

"Certainly," the doctor agreed as he rose to check on another patient. "Just don't stay long. She's extremely weak."

Roy slipped down the hall and through the door to Edith's room. When he sat next to the bed, Edith opened her dark brown eyes and turned her head toward him. A faint smile spread across her lips.

"Hello, Edith," he greeted her softly as he took her hand in his. "How are you feeling?"

"Not too well," she whispered. "I feel like I've been run over by a steam roller."

"The air ambulance will be here in a few minutes to take you to Great Falls Deaconess. I'm going to drive to Great Falls to be with you and to meet Jean's flight tonight."

"Thanks for everything." Edith's eyes closed as she loosened her grasp on his hand.

"Don't worry about a thing. You have the best medical care available. I'll see you in a couple hours in Great Falls." With that he leaned over and gave her a quick kiss on the forehead then quietly left the room. A trip to Great Falls was the least he could do for the one who was beginning to mean so much to him.

Two hours later Roy approached the admissions desk in the main lobby of Deaconess Hospital. "What is

Edith Harkness's room number? She arrived about an hour ago by air ambulance from Rocky Bluff."

"Just a moment, please," the receptionist responded as she typed the name into the computer on her desk. "She's in Acute Cardiac Care Unit Number Three on the third floor. Please check at the nursing station on that floor."

Roy thanked the woman and hurried to catch the waiting elevator. Approaching the cardiac care nursing station, he was overwhelmed with the number of monitors with lines pulsing up and down. The nurse on duty did not look up from the screens as he approached. He waited in silence a few moments before a much younger nurse appeared from a small drug chamber nearby. She locked the door behind herself and placed the key in her pocket.

"May I help you?"

"Yes, I'm here to see Edith Harkness who arrived from Rocky Bluff."

"You must be Roy Dutton," she responded with a smile. "We've been expecting you. The flight attendants told us that you would be coming as a representative of the family. Edith is in ACCU Number Three, but they just took her down to have a heart cath. It'll be another hour to an hour and a half before she'll be back in her room. You may wait in her room, the visitors' lounge, or in the cafeteria on the main floor."

Roy felt disappointed that he couldn't see Edith right away. "I didn't have any breakfast before I left this morning so I think I'll catch a quick bite to eat in the cafeteria."

Roy found a table in the hospital dining hall beside a

window.   He relaxed with a bowl of ham and bean soup and a chef's salad. With each bite he felt his strength renewed. His body ached from lack of sleep and tension. After forty-five minutes of watching the hospital employees and the visitors come and go, he returned to the third floor to wait for word about Edith.

Stepping off the elevator, Roy greeted the staff at the nurses' station and tried to make himself comfortable in the lounge. He scanned the magazines on the table and picked up a few current issues but the minutes dragged by. Finally a gurney appeared, pushed by two muscular orderlies dressed in green. Roy rose to meet them.

"The doctor will be here shortly to talk with you," the taller one explained as Roy neared the gurney. "We'll have Mrs. Harkness settled in her bed in a few minutes."

Roy paced nervously up and down the hallway until a balding doctor stopped him at the end of the hall. "Mr. Dutton?" he questioned, offering his hand in greeting. "I'm Dr. Pierce."

"It's nice to meet you," Roy responded. "I'm a good friend of Edith Harkness. How is she?"

"It's a miracle that she's still alive. She's quite a fighter." The doctor motioned for him to join him in the visitors' lounge. "Has any of her family arrived yet?"

"They won't be in until this evening. Her daughter is coming from Idaho tonight and her son is coming from Rocky Bluff in the morning. Is Edith going to be all right?"

"Mrs. Harkness suffered a serious cardiac arrest. The

main artery into the heart is 95 percent blocked; another artery is 90 percent blocked and another 82 percent blocked. I've scheduled her for open-heart surgery first thing in the morning. I'll have her family finish signing the necessary papers as soon as they arrive. Edith has already signed the release to do surgery, but she is much too weak to question further."

"What are her chances of resuming a normal lifestyle?" Roy questioned with a worried sigh.

"I can't give you any percentages. She appears to be strong and in good health otherwise. We have an excellent staff of heart surgeons so she has much in her favor. Many of our patients are back to their normal routines within three months, but each case is different."

The doctor paused, trying not to generate false optimism. "Edith's situation is extremely serious, however. I'll keep you posted on her condition and will talk more with you and the family after the surgery tomorrow."

After the doctor disappeared down the hallway, Roy sat in the visitors' lounge in stunned silence for nearly a half-hour. Although he knew there was a strong possibility of surgery when he came to Great Falls, the harsh reality of the situation sent cold chills down his spine. Finally he slipped quietly into Edith's room. While he stood beside her sleeping form an assurance of peace settled over him. In spite of the formidable circumstances, God still had everything under control.

Regaining his emotional equilibrium, Roy left the hospital to find accommodations. Less than a block away he spotted a modest motel with a flashing neon sign, Sunrise Inn. He parked the car in front and stepped into a clean, efficient office. "May I help you?" the manager greeted.

"I'd like to reserve three rooms for at least two nights. I need a single for Jean Thompson, a double for Bob Harkness, and I'll need a single for myself. My name is Roy Dutton."

"That will be no problem, Mr. Dutton." The manager smiled as she checked the register.

"We have a friend and family member who is going to have surgery in the morning." Roy explained, reaching into his pocket for his wallet.

"We serve many of the patients' families. You can let me know in the morning how long you'll be staying." The office manager hurriedly took down the necessary information and filled out the credit card forms. "Here are the keys to your rooms. I hope you enjoy your stay."

Roy kept the key to room 116 and dropped the other two into the pocket of his suitcoat. After he unlocked the door and hung his suitcoat on the back of a chair, he removed his tie and shoes and stretched out on the bed. A few hours of rest seemed extremely inviting to his weary body.

Later that evening Roy anxiously drove the quiet streets of the city to the Great Falls International Airport. He had seen several pictures of Jean but he had never met her in person. Only a handful of maintenance people and baggage personnel were there to greet the arriving passengers. Finally the loudspeaker blared, "Horizon Flight Number 315 is now arriving at Gate

Number 2."

Roy jumped to his feet and waited as the passengers began to file by the checkstand. After a few moments a tall, dark-haired young woman began walking toward him.

"Are you Roy Dutton?" she asked confidently.

"Yes, and you must be Jean. You look just like your photos."

"It's nice to meet you, Roy. I've heard so many good things about you." As she extended her right hand, Roy noted how much her mannerisms were like her mother's. "How is Mother? I've been extremely worried about her."

"They did a heart cath today, and she's scheduled to have three by-passes first thing in the morning," Roy explained as he picked up her suitcase from the luggage checkstand. "The doctor says she's in extremely good health for someone her age and the finest heart surgeons I'm told are on staff. The doctor would like to have you check in at the business office and the nurses' station as soon as you arrive at the hospital. There are still some forms that need to be signed."

"There's always so much paper work at hospitals," she sighed. "I think I spend more time at work filling out forms than caring for the patients. Anyway, I appreciate your coming to be with Mother and to pick me up. Did you think to make a reservation at a motel for me?"

"Yes, at the Sunrise Inn, nothing fancy but comfortable and only a block from the hospital. Bob will be here first thing in the morning and his room is waiting whenever he arrives."

Later, alone in his motel room, Roy read his Bible, but his mind could only concentrate on his dearest friend lying weak and vulnerable in a strange hospital room. *At least God understands the needs and desires of my heart,* he thought as he closed his Bible. He turned off the bedside lamp and resigned himself to another night of fitful sleep.

eight

Roy was up at dawn and went directly to the hospital. He stopped at the nurses' station to inquire about Edith's condition.

"Mrs. Harkness has already been given her pre-op medications and she's a little groggy. I can tell you that she rested well through the night and did not have any further problems," the head nurse assured him. "The surgical procedure generally takes about five hours and we try to keep the family informed as to the progress of the surgery. You may stop in her room and see her but don't stay long. There's a family room down the hall if you care to wait."

"Thank you for your kindness. Her daughter and son should be along shortly."

As Roy turned, Bob and Nancy appeared. "How's Mom?" Bob demanded abruptly.

"They said she had a good night's rest and they will be taking her to surgery in a few minutes. Jean should be here any time now. She had to stop at the business office."

"I'm sure everything will be all right," the younger man replied stiffly. "Thank you for coming ahead to be with Mother. If you want to go back to Rocky Bluff, I think we can handle it for a few days. I know Jean has taken a temporary leave of absence from work."

"That's all right. I didn't come this far to leave your

mother now. I'll stay until she's better."

"Whatever you like, but I'd hate to have our family problems interfere with your personal life."

Just then Jean entered the waiting room. The few hours of sleep seemed to have refreshed her. "How's Mother this morning?"

Bob stood in detached silence while Roy answered. "Your mother is almost ready to go to surgery," he explained softly. "They have given her a shot so she's a little groggy, but I'm sure she'll want to see you."

The family walked toward Edith's room. Roy politely pushed the door open for Jean. She was professionally trained to deal with critically ill patients, but she was not emotionally equipped to deal with her mother lying in a sterile hospital room. She choked back her tears as she approached the bed. Edith roused and turned her head toward her daughter. A faint smile spread across her face. "Jean, what a surprise," she whispered. "When did you get here?"

"I flew in late last night. Roy met me at the airport." Jean took her mother's hand in hers. "I plan to stay until you're able to take care of yourself again. While I'm gone Jim is prepared to hold down the fort as long as necessary. You get some rest now and remember, we are all here with you."

Bob and Nancy stuck their heads into the room. "I know there is a limit of two visitors per patient, but can we have a quick prayer with Mother before she goes to surgery?" Nancy asked.

"Please do," Edith murmured as Roy walked around the bed and took her other hand.

The four together said a simple prayer for healing,

comfort, and strength. As they were whispering their Amens, two orderlies appeared in the doorway. "Are you ready, Mrs. Harkness?" one of them asked as Jean stepped aside to allow the gurney to be wheeled next to the bed.

"As ready as I'll ever be," Edith responded weakly.

"Our prayers are with you, Mom," Jean said as the family turned to leave the room.

As soon as the gurney was pushed onto the elevator Bob turned to Nancy. "Let's go downtown for breakfast. Hospitals are too depressing for me and besides, the surgery takes five hours and we can be back by noon. Anyway, there are some supplies I want to check on with the wholesaler."

Anger flashed through Nancy's dark brown eyes. She took a quivering breath. "There's a cafeteria right here in the hospital. Surely business can wait until your mother's surgery is over?"

"There's nothing we can do here. I need to get outside and get some fresh air. Let's at least go downtown for breakfast and come back as soon as we've eaten."

Nancy turned to her sister-in-law with an embarrassed look. "Would you excuse us for a bit? We'll meet you here later. I'm anxious to hear all about the plans for my future niece."

"Or nephew," Jean corrected as Bob and Nancy disappeared down the hospital corridor. Shocked by her brother's lack of concern, Jean stood in silence with tears building in her eyes. Suddenly she began to sob. Roy wrapped his long arms around her in a fatherly manner as she buried her face in his sweater. The time when she felt that she should be the strongest she found herself crumbling like a little girl. The thought of the woman who had loved and nurtured her all her life lying on a surgeon's table had rendered her temporarily helpless.

After a few minutes the tears stopped and Jean felt emotionally drained. Roy gave her a warm smile. "Let's go down to the cafeteria and have some breakfast. A cup of coffee and some toast will do us both good."

A friendship grew between Roy and Jean as they sat across the table from each other. Although they had met only the night before, they were bound together by a common concern.

Roy spread grape jelly on his toast and looked up at the young woman so like her mother. "You must be extremely close to Edith," he shrewdly observed.

"Much more than most mothers and daughters," Jean replied, relieved to have an opportunity to talk about her mother with someone who was also concerned. "We were among the few who made the transition from a parent-child relationship to an adult friendship. I can truthfully say that except for my husband, my mother is my best friend."

"She's a remarkable woman. You should hear her compassion and wisdom when she talks to crisis line callers. The depth of her character is astounding."

"It's too bad that Bob hasn't developed that relationship with Mother. After she retired he treated her as if she were a total invalid, of no value except to serve as a source of a sizeable inheritance."

Jean sighed with disgust. "I may be judging him wrong, but I get the feeling that his basic philosophy is life ends at sixty, so get all you can while you're young."

"That's a pretty miserable perception. You know, most people haven't discovered that the best part of life can be the retirement years."

"I'm beginning to understand what you mean. Sometimes I think that by the time we finally learn how to live the way God intended, our lives are almost over."

"Well, the nicest thing about being old is that you don't have to worry about getting old anymore," Roy chuckled as he pushed his plate aside and leaned back in his chair.

The two continued a lively conversation about world events and personal problems, staying in the cafeteria long after their meal was over. Occasionally Roy's eyes strayed to the scene outside the nearby window. A park-like courtyard was in the center of the hospital complex. "Let's go outside for a walk and get some fresh air and then go upstairs and see if there is any word from the operating room."

Jean stood up, pushed her chair under the table, and followed him out the cafeteria door. Slowly the two strolled around the tree-lined sidewalk that encircled the hospital. The spring morning reinforced their hope and faith that Edith would be restored to complete health. The God who created such a beautiful world could rebuild a damaged heart. But would He?

Around ten o'clock Jean and Roy returned to the third-floor waiting room, although they knew it might be another hour before they received word on the surgery. Much to their surprise they were greeted by Nancy and Bob.

"Where have you been?" Bob demanded as soon as

he spotted his sister. "I thought you of all people—a nurse!—would be staying here in case someone came with a report on Mother."

Jean's temper flared as she tried to ignore his outburst. "We've been for a walk around the hospital."

Nancy shuffled nervously and reached out and took her sister-in-law's arm. "Jean, come tell me all about your plans for the baby. I'm so excited for you."

As the women attempted to engage in talk of babies and homes, the men each picked up a magazine and thumbed through the pages, neither acknowledging the presence of the other.

"It's nearly eleven o'clock. We should be hearing about Mother's progress soon," Jean observed half to herself and half to the others. "I'm sure everything is going okay. The doctors doing the surgery are highly respected by the medical people in Chamberland, but that still doesn't remove my fears."

Bob began to pace the floor. He paused before the open window for several minutes, admiring the sights of the city below and the majestic Highwood Mountains that silhouetted the horizon. Although no one spoke, the tension mounted in the small waiting room.

At eleven-thirty a nurse appeared in the doorway. "Are you the family of Edith Harkness?"

"Yes, I'm her daughter, Jean. How is she?"

"The surgery is taking a little longer than expected, but everything is under control. She should be out of surgery in another hour or so," the nurse assured them.

"It shouldn't be taking this long for three bypasses," Jean responded, the creases in her forehead deepening. "Are there complications?"

doctors like you."

"Let me know if there are any problems or questions concerning your mother," Dr. Pierce told them as he rose to leave.

"Whew! I'm glad that's over and Mother is holding her own," Bob said after a few minutes' silence as they all absorbed the doctor's news. "Now I can get back to work at the store by tomorrow if Jean's going to stay here. It's a busy time of year with the lawn and garden supplies just starting to sell."

All faces registered shock at Bob's blasé attitude. "As I said earlier," Jean replied tartly, "I plan to stay until Mother is home and able to care for herself."

Bob turned to Roy. "I assume you'll be going home tonight as well."

"No, Bob. I have enough trained volunteers to run the crisis phone for two or three weeks without a problem."

"Whatever you think, but I'm sure Jean can handle everything here. After all, she's a nurse by profession." Bob gave the last words an almost sarcastic emphasis.

"I'm sure Mother will enjoy his company while she's recovering," Nancy inserted, trying to break another tension-filled situation initiated by her husband. Without scarcely taking a breath Nancy turned her attention to her sister-in-law. "Please cancel our reservations at the motel. I guess we won't be using them after all. If you need any help just give me a call and I'll come right back."

"Thanks, I appreciate your offer. Roy and I will keep you posted on her progress."

Nancy gave her sister-in-law a quick hug as Bob

hurried toward the door, expecting his wife to follow instinctively. Jean and Roy watched as the pair disappeared down the hall and entered the waiting elevator. As they sat together in silence, Roy observed from Jean's body language her barely suppressed anger at Bob's seemingly callous behavior.

"Jean, I don't mean to pry, but does Bob have a reason to resent my friendship with your mother?" Roy asked as he surveyed the attractive young woman who sat across from him.

"Truthfully, Bob has become nothing more than a greedy, self-centered slob. Although he's my only brother, I'm beginning to see him in a totally different light. Money is fast becoming his god."

"Those are pretty harsh words, but I've also observed a preoccupation with money. Maybe that's his problem. He probably thinks I'm only interested in your mother's money."

"Anything is possible. He's really becoming touchy about the store's future. Maybe when this is all over we can have a good talk with Bob. Everyone is becoming extremely sensitive to his attitude, but we all try to sweep it under the carpet and pretend that nothing is wrong."

"I'm sure it's not beyond hope," Roy assured her. "In spite of his outward expression of disinterest in his mother I sense a real love and protectiveness underneath. The good side of Bob will eventually win out."

A smile spread across Jean's face as the tension lines relaxed. "I certainly hope you're right."

"Let's go to the acute cardiac unit and see your mother. I'll feel better just seeing her again even if she's sleeping." Roy gestured for Jean to follow him.

Edith lay motionless surrounded by tubes and monitors. Her gray-flecked hair framed her pale but serene face. They studied the scene for several moments in silence. Finally Jean spoke. "She's in good hands. Maybe we should go now."

Roy retired to the motel for some needed rest, which he admitted he had done without since Edith became ill. Jean decided to stay at the hospital, her only companions a few books and a troubled heart.

The days passed slowly for Jean and Roy as they kept a constant vigil at Edith's bedside. Within three days the doctors felt she was strong enough to move into a semiprivate room on the cardiac care floor. Due to the complications of the surgery Edith did not regain her strength as fast as the medical team would have liked, but her positive attitude and a sustaining faith kept her constantly moving forward. Every day Nancy called Jean at the motel to inquire about her mother-in-law. Bob, however, was always busy at the store.

"Mother, some flowers just arrived," Jean said brightly as she set a beautiful arrangement of yellow and pink carnations on her nightstand.

"Who are they from?" Edith murmured, a smile spreading across her face.

"The card says, 'From your son, Bob'," Jean replied as she noted a sadness in her mother's eyes.

"Isn't there even a note attached? I've been here over a week."

"I'm sorry, Mom. Just the flowers arrived. I'm sure Bob must be very busy this time of year."

Nothing more was said about the lack of support from Bob, but there seemed an emptiness in the family. Hopefully, things would be different when Edith returned to Rocky Bluff.

After two weeks of taking turns sitting at Edith's bedside, Roy and Jean began talking more and more about Edith's homecoming. As they talked, Edith's spirits lifted but a sense of helplessness kept invading her speech. "I guess I don't have a heart like a twenty year old anymore. A year ago Dr. Brewer told me that I did, but now I'm beginning to wonder if I'll ever be able to take care of myself."

"Don't worry about a thing, Mom. I'm planning to stay with you until you can," Jean assured her as she took her hand.

"You don't want to be apart from your husband too long," Edith protested weakly. "That's not good for any marriage. The doctor said that I won't be able to climb the stairs to the bedroom for some time."

"Roy and I have been talking about that," Jean stated calmly. "We could convert the den into a bedroom."

"You know, I've been thinking about that too." Edith adjusted her bed to an upright position with the automatic controls. "The furniture shouldn't be too difficult to move, but I'd want to keep the bookcase and my sewing machine in the den."

"I'll tell you what," Roy began, rubbing his chin thoughtfully. "Why don't I go back to Rocky Bluff tomorrow and rearrange the furniture? I can get a couple of kids from the school to help me. You won't have to worry about a thing. If you don't like where I hang the pictures and place the knickknacks, I can move them again when you get home."

Edith's eyes filled with tears. "That would be kind of you. Maybe Bob would help, if he's not too busy at the store. May is a such a busy time with the last-minute shopping for gardening supplies."

"Oh, I don't mind doing this at all. I'll get your bedroom ready and then as soon as the doctor says you can come home I'll drive back and get you and Jean. You're fortunate to have such a fine nurse for a daughter, or should I say such a fine daughter for a nurse? I imagine Dr. Pierce will let you come home earlier than normal just because of Jean."

True to his word, Roy spent the next few days rearranging Edith's house, occasionally with Nancy's help. When he received word that the doctor was going to dismiss Edith the following day he called Nancy to relay the news.

"I'll be over this evening," she promised. "I want to make the bed and be sure that all the linens are handy. Maybe I'll pick up some groceries on my way. Jean's going to have enough to do caring for Mother without having to worry about the shopping for a few days."

That night Nancy and the children joined Roy at Edith's house. Jay and Dawn painted a "Welcome Home, Grandma" banner and hung it in the front window. They could scarcely contain their excitement at the prospect of seeing their grandmother again.

Roy left early the next morning for Great Falls. The miles of newly sprouting wheat fields flew by as the warmth of the bright spring morning enveloped him. His prayers had been answered: Edith was returning home.

When Roy arrived at the hospital Jean had already helped her mother dress and she was sitting in the chair beside the bed. She had also fixed her mother's hair and helped her with her make-up. The sight of Edith looking so well uplifted Roy's spirits and he was sure she would completely recover.

Three hours later as they stopped in front of Edith's house they began to giggle. Jay and Dawn's banner completely covered the full length of Edith's picture window.

"One thing I'm blessed with is a loving family and good friends. I don't know what I'd have done without each of you," Edith said as tears of gratitude filled her eyes.

Roy opened the car door and offered Edith his arm. Slowly they made their way up the sidewalk. "I've been in the hospital so long my legs feel like rubber," Edith complained as Roy wrapped his arm around her to help support more of her weight.

"Just a few more steps and we'll have it made," he assured her as he unlocked the front door. Roy helped Edith into the bedroom while Jean followed closely behind with her mother's suitcase. "Well, what do you think?" Roy asked, pleased as a young boy bringing home his first A.

Speechless, Edith turned to give him a big thank-you kiss. Wiping a tear from her eyes, she managed, "Even the pictures are hung exactly where I would have put them myself."

"Then I think I'll run on home and leave you in the competent hands of Nurse Jean. You need to get to bed and get some rest."

"Thanks again for all you've done," Edith replied as Roy leaned over to kiss her goodbye. "I am a little weary."

When school was out that afternoon Jay and Dawn hurried to their grandmother's house. "Hi, Aunt Jean. Can we see Grandma?" they begged as soon as she opened the door.

Jean gave her niece and nephew a quick hug. "She'll be glad to see you, but be real quiet, she's awfully tired."

Jay and Dawn tiptoed into their grandmother's bedroom. Edith heard them and rolled over. "Come here, both of you, so I can give you a hug." Edith sat up and gave each of her grandchildren a weak embrace. "I really missed you when I was in the hospital."

"I'm glad you're home," Jay said as he squeezed his grandmother. "Did you like our banner?"

"I loved it," Edith assured them. "It was the best welcome home I ever had." The children beamed with pride as Jean entered the bedroom.

"I hate to break up the party, but I think we'd better let Grandma get her rest. I have some cookies and milk in the kitchen," Jean said as she motioned for the children to follow her.

"'Bye, Grandma," Jay and Dawn echoed in unison as they followed their aunt to the kitchen.

Edith leaned back with contentment. It was good to be home. She was determined to do her exercises and follow her doctors' orders explicitly so that she could regain her strength. She'd already set her goal to be well by the Fourth of July. Sharing the church's annual picnic with her family had always been—and would continue to be—the highlight of her summer.

nine

After Roy returned from Great Falls he was anxious to see his son, hopeful that time would have healed their strained relationship. Through the weeks of concern for Edith, the tension with his son had been pushed into the background.

The last weekend of every month the Davidsons took Pete to a nearby town where he caught the noon bus for Rocky Bluff. The following Tuesday they would meet him at the depot and take him back to the ranch.

Friday afternoon Roy nervously waited for the five o'clock bus. When the double-decker finally pulled to a stop Pete was, as usual, the first to get off. "Hi, Dad," he greeted, giving his father a quick embrace.

"Pete, it's good to have you home. Let me get your luggage for you." Roy breathed a sigh of relief that his son seemed to be his normal, bubbly self.

"Can we stop at McDonald's before we go home? I'm starving."

"Good idea." Driving down the main street of Rocky Bluff, Roy turned to his son. "How's the ranch work coming along this month?"

"The planting's done. A lot of the equipment broke down so I've been busy in the shop most of the time."

"You can fix almost anything, can't you?" Roy parked the car in the only slot left in the parking lot.

"Once I had trouble getting a transmission back in

104

their half-ton truck. I never worked on that kind before. It was really hard, but I finally got it in and running."

They ate in silence in a corner booth until Pete finished his first Big Mac. "Dad, why did you go to Great Falls when Edith was sick?"

"I wanted to be with her and try to make her as happy as possible."

"The doctors and nurses are there to take care of people. Why did you need to be there?"

"It's pretty lonesome to be in a hospital in a city where you don't know anyone."

"Didn't her family go to see her?"

"Her daughter Jean and I took turns staying in the room with her. I think we were a big comfort to her. Would you like to go visit Edith this weekend while you're home?"

"No way! I don't want anything to do with her. You shouldn't either."

"Pete, don't you think there's enough love in my heart for two people? I've found that the more love I give away, the more I have to give."

Totally unconvinced, Pete's cheerfulness turned to gloom and he finished his second hamburger in silence. Pete's thoughts turned to the one person who seemed to understand his dilemma. *Maybe Bob has thought of some way to keep them apart. . .he doesn't want them to see each other either.*

Pete spent the remaining hours of the day in front of the TV. At ten o'clock he switched off the set and headed for his bedroom without saying good night to Roy.

Roy watched his son with anguish as he disappeared down the hall. He picked up a sports magazine from the coffee table and scanned the pages without focusing on the words.

The following morning Roy was up early to fix a breakfast of bacon, eggs, toast, juice, and milk. Pete ate his double portion in silence and then got up from the table and headed for the door.

"Where are you going, Pete?"

"For a little walk," he mumbled, not turning around. Roy watched the door close behind him. He and his son had been the closest of friends only a few months before. Now they acted like strangers.

Outside the well-kept bungalow Pete took a deep breath. He needed help. He had to stop his father's friendship with Edith before they got married.

Pete increased his pace as he neared the business section of Rocky Bluff. Rounding the corner on Main Street, he entered Harkness Hardware and found the manager sitting at his desk in the back of the store. "Hi, Bob," he began weakly, afraid that Bob might have forgotten the talk they had a few weeks before.

When Bob looked up from his desk his face broke into a broad smile. "Well, hello, Pete. Welcome home. What brings you out so early in the morning?"

"I wanted to talk to you."

"Good. I've been wanting to visit with you as well. Let's go across the street and have some coffee."

Bob put his hand on Pete's shoulder as they stepped outside. "There's no problem that the two of us can't figure out together," he said grinning.

"I hope so," Pete replied with his customary slow

drawl. He felt better already. Bob seemed to be able to handle any situation that arose, even an enormous problem like the one he faced.

"What's on your mind today, Pete?" Bob asked as the waitress brought two steaming cups of coffee.

"My dad is still seeing your mother. It's worse than ever. You said you'd help me keep them apart but he went to Great Falls when she was in the hospital. Maybe they'll get married and forget me."

"My mother is so sick that marriage would be the last thing on her mind."

In spite of his own reassuring words, Bob had his doubts. *What if Roy thinks she won't last much longer and tries to marry her to get his hands on my father's estate?* Lost in his thoughts, Bob had temporarily forgotten the young man sitting across the table.

Pete waited impatiently as Bob stared blankly out the drugstore window. Finally he demanded, "What are you thinking about, Bob? Do you have any ideas on how to keep them apart?"

"I just had an idea but I don't know if it will work. Would you be able to talk your father into taking an extended vacation with you? Maybe going to Europe or someplace like that?"

"Go to Europe?" Pete asked excitedly. "That's way across the ocean. That would cost too much money."

"Maybe I could come up with some money for the plane tickets, but it'd have to be a secret between the two of us." Bob watched the look of eagerness on Pete's face. "I have an old army buddy who now heads a travel agency in Germany. When we were in Vietnam I helped carry him out from behind enemy lines when he was wounded. He owes me a favor."

Pete looked puzzled. "But how can he help?"

"Maybe he'll be able to arrange free room and board and book you on some of the local tours. "

"Do you really mean you'd help my dad and me go to Europe? Colorado is the farthest I've ever been. I've never even been on an airplane."

"Sure," Bob replied confidently. "Then you could have your father all to yourself. Why don't you tell your dad to come to the store about two-thirty this afternoon and talk to me about the trip? You can tell him I want to repay him for staying with Mother while she was in the hospital."

A few minutes later Pete burst through the living room door of the Dutton residence. "Did you have a good walk?" Roy asked as he looked up from the desk where he was balancing his checkbook. It was obvious that his son's mood had improved considerably.

"This wasn't a normal walk," Pete exclaimed, flopping onto the sofa and stretching his long legs under the coffee table in front of him. "We might get to go to Europe for free. They had a show on TV the other night about Europe and I really want to go."

"What does a free trip to Europe have to do with your walk?" Roy queried with amusement. Pete would often become excited and then be unable to separate his desires from reality. Years of experience had taught Roy not to challenge Pete's dreams directly.

Pete was puzzled over his father's lack of excitement about a trip to Europe. "I'm serious, Dad. Bob Harkness said that he'd take care of everything for us."

"Is the hardware store having a drawing for some

lucky couple to win a trip to Europe? I've never been lucky at anything like that."

"Oh, no, nothing like that. Bob says that he owes you a favor for staying with his mother while she was in the hospital. He wants you to come to the store this afternoon and talk to him."

One word tumbled on top of the other as his simple mind tried to keep the real reason for the trip separate from the story Bob wanted him to tell his father. "Please, Dad, let's go to the store this afternoon and talk about it."

"There must be something else involved. I'll go talk to Bob and get this straightened out. People don't offer free trips to Europe to just anybody. But before I go to the store I'd like to run over and see how Edith's feeling today. Do you want to come with me?"

"No, Dad!" Pete objected as his face reddened with anger. "This is the only time I have to be with you. I want you to play checkers with me. We haven't done that in a long time."

"Maybe I could play one quick game before I go. Do you want to get the checkerboard?"

But after a quick game Pete was still not satisfied. "How about two out of three?"

Usually Roy let Pete win a game now and then, but this time he made sure he won so that the games would be short. As much as he loved his son, he did not want Pete to keep him from seeing Edith, especially now.

After losing a second game Pete suggested a third one, but Roy was already putting the checkers in the box. Realizing that he would be unable to keep his father from seeing Edith, Pete decided to join him. He didn't want Edith to have him completely to herself for the afternoon.

Jean answered the door dressed in faded blue jeans and a plaid maternity top. "Roy, how good to see you again. Mother will be delighted."

"Jean, I'd like you to meet my son Pete. He came home to be with me for the weekend."

"How do you do, Pete? I've heard many good things about you. Won't you come in and sit down? Mother will be out in just a minute."

Pete slouched in the rocking chair by the window and began thumbing through a sporting goods catalog beside him, completely ignoring the others in the room.

"Jean, before your mother gets here do you know anything about Bob offering Pete and me a free trip to Europe? Pete came home this morning with the report that Bob had a friend in Germany who was willing to provide room and board for us for several weeks. Bob said he wanted to pay me back for staying at the hospital with your mother by providing us with the plane tickets."

Jean looked at Roy in amazement. *Surely Pete must have misunderstood,* she thought. "Bob has never been generous with money. I don't understand why he would start now."

"Does he really have a friend in Germany who'd be willing to do all of that for a total stranger?"

"Well, he did save a guy's life in Vietnam, and has taken advantage of him ever since. This man went to Germany right after he finished his tour of duty and now he runs a large hotel and travel service. Beyond that I don't know much about him."

Just then Edith appeared in the doorway. "Roy, Pete, I'm glad you both came. Has Jean offered you a cup of coffee yet?"

"I'm sorry. We got busy talking and I forgot," Jean apologized. "Can I get you both a cup?"

"Certainly," Roy replied as he joined Edith on the sofa.

"How about you, Pete?" Jean asked.

"None for me," he answered, not looking up from the automotive section of the catalog. He was confused by Jean's response to her brother's generous offer. *How could she say that? Bob was such a nice guy. He's the only one who understands me. He knows that Dad and Edith don't belong together.*

Edith, Jean, and Roy talked about the upcoming vote to raise the mill levy in order to build a new wing on the high school. Pete sat in the rocking chair and sulked. Contempt for the former school teacher grew with each passing minute. Finally Pete couldn't stand it any longer. "Dad, let's go down to the hardware store and see Bob. I told him we'd be in around two- thirty."

"In a few minutes, son," Roy responded kindly. "We still have plenty of time."

Pete slouched deeper into the chair, his chin resting on his chest. He kept his eyes fixed on the grandfather clock in the corner. At exactly two-twenty-five Pete spoke again. "Please, Dad. I don't want to keep Bob waiting."

"All right, son," Roy answered reluctantly, joining him at the door.

"I'll see you later, Edith. Thanks for the coffee." Roy looked back at his dear friend dressed in a bright red lounging robe. The vivid color formed an attractive contrast against her hair. A smile spread across his face as their eyes met. "Take care of yourself."

"Don't be too disappointed if I turn down the offer to go to Europe," Roy told his son as he started the engine of the car. "It's not that I don't want to go, but I don't want to be away from Edith very long until the doctor has given her a clean bill of health. I also don't want to feel indebted to a stranger in Germany, much less to Bob. I hope you understand that."

The meeting between Roy and Bob was brief. Bob's explanation of the trip as payment for staying with Edith sounded suspicious to Roy. He did not want to be paid for helping someone whom he had grown to love.

"I appreciate your offer, Bob, but I can't accept it. I cannot take any more time away from the Crisis Center, and besides, I don't want to leave your mother until the doctor says she can resume normal activities," Roy explained as Pete sat beside him scowling. He thanked Bob again for his offer and left the store with Pete shuffling dejectedly behind him.

Frustrated that his initial plan did not work, Bob soon developed another. A few days later he stopped to visit his mother after work. "Mom, now that your health is failing have you ever considered selling this big house?" he began as he paced nervously in front of the window. "Rocky Bluff has several openings at their senior citizens housing project. It'd be much wiser to plan for your financial future instead of waiting until you're desperate and are forced to take the only options left available."

"I don't want to give up this house," Edith protested

adamantly. "I've lived in this house since I was married. Why should I leave it now after I finally got it paid for and fixed the way I like it?"

"It's too big for you to care for. Jean will have to go back to Idaho soon and you won't be able to keep it up. We could arrange a trust fund to take care of your future medical bills and also a fund for your grandchildren's education. Financial planning is the name of the game these days. I could oversee the entire plan myself so you wouldn't have to worry about a thing."

"The answer is no, and I do not want to hear anything more about it."

Jean was aghast at her brother's suggestion. Concerned that her mother was getting too excited, Jean immediately changed the subject to her expectant state. Nothing pleased Edith more than the thought of another grandchild. She was proud of the two she already had and prospects that a third one was on the way brought only joy.

Thwarted in his scheme, Bob soon found an excuse to leave. As he walked down the steps Jean turned to her mother. "This is a terrible thing to say about my own brother, but how did he ever get a saintly wife like Nancy?"

"You're right, Jean. It's not nice to say," Edith scolded gently. "Maybe someday the good Lord will be able to help Bob straighten out his priorities. Bob really has some good points and he is my son, but I'm afraid he's too involved in trying to make as much money as possible in the least amount of time."

Yet what worried Edith most was that Bob was fast becoming his own worst enemy.

ten

As Edith rested in her recliner at the picture window, her thoughts were centered on her garden plot in the backyard, especially the lush and aromatic lilac bushes. Ever since her marriage to George Harkness her summer days had been occupied with gardening. This summer, however, her garden would have to fend for itself. She was not willing to ask her pregnant daughter or her daughter-in-law to help her.

Jean suddenly interrupted her mother's train of thought. "It's beautiful outside. How about taking your walk a little earlier today?"

"Even if I can't work in my garden at least I can still enjoy the out of doors," Edith replied as Jean helped her with her sweater.

Slowly Edith and Jean descended the steps and made their way down the main sidewalk. They paused when they reached the end of the block. "Do you think there is any way I can go to church tomorrow?" Edith asked. "I've really missed it. Sunday just isn't Sunday without being in church."

"We'll try it," Jean promised as they turned and headed back to the house. "I can park the car in the handicap parking space and you can use the wheelchair ramp so you won't have to climb those steep front stairs. We'll slip out during the last hymn so you won't get caught in the crowd."

"When they remodeled the church five years ago I didn't realize how important the changes for the handicapped would be until I needed to use them myself," Edith admitted, remembering all the discussions that went on about the ramp at that time. "If there's one thing I've learned through all of this, it's to be more sensitive to others."

The next morning Jean and Edith arrived at church twenty minutes early. Edith felt alert and invigorated by her first outing since her hospitalization. The warm Montana sun reflected off the golden steeple cross while a robin chirped happily from its crossbar.

"I wish I had my camera right now," Edith observed. "Because of that robin I know God still has everything under control."

During the last hymn Jean and Edith slipped out the side door. Once home Edith promptly changed into a lounging robe and stretched out on her bed with a smile of contentment on her face.

Later that afternoon Edith and Roy had time alone while Jean visited Bonnie, a former high school classmate. The couple sat in relaxed silence for a few moments. Finally Roy cleared his throat. "Edith, have you ever considered remarrying?"

Edith looked up with surprise. "I guess I've never given it much thought. After George died I devoted all my efforts and time to my students. Why do you ask?"

"I thought I was content living the life of a single man until I met you. As the months have passed I'm more and more convinced that I'd like to share the rest of my life with you."

As their eyes met Edith had to admit the feeling was

mutual although she had never verbalized it. Yet it wasn't practical. "Roy, how can you say that, with my health lingering in the balance as it is. You don't want to spend the rest of your days caring for an invalid."

"But Edith, yours is not a permanent condition," Roy protested mildly. "Each day you're able to walk farther than you did the day before. It won't be long before you'll be walking around the block. In a few weeks you should be as good as new."

"I wish that were true." She paused and cleared her throat. "At my last check-up the doctor said there had been some permanent damage to my heart and I should avoid all strenuous activities. I'll have to ignore the fact that I have an upstairs and a basement in my house."

Roy said took her hand lovingly. "We all have certain physical limitations. In a few weeks you'll be self-sufficient again and life won't seem nearly as dismal. I love you for what you are, not for what your body can or can't do."

"Roy, if only we'd met ten years ago things might be different," Edith sighed, tears glistening in her eyes.

"No self-pity allowed," Roy scolded kindly. "Have you already forgotten what Pastor Rhodes said in his sermon? We're to live one day at a time and we're to live it to the fullest."

"You're right," Edith confessed, forcing a smile. "I'm being rather silly, but marriage is a big step. Let's think about it a while longer and see how fast I get my strength back."

When the next Sunday arrived, Edith was up early dressing for church. She had always considered her faith in Jesus Christ important, but now after her surgery she realized that she could not survive without the Lord's sustaining hand.

Following the morning worship service she greeted Pastor Rhodes at the door. "You can't imagine how good it is to be back in church. It seems to make my entire week go better."

"I'm glad you're able to get out again. I saw you here last week but you slipped out before I had a chance to talk to you. If you're not busy Tuesday afternoon, I'll come by and visit for a few minutes."

"I'll have the coffee pot waiting." Edith moved out the side door as Pastor Rhodes turned his attention to the next person in line.

Tuesday as Jean was finishing the noon dishes the phone rang. She reached around the corner of the cupboard and picked up the receiver. "Hello, Harkness residence."

"Hello, is Jean Thompson available please?" a woman asked in a pleasant, businesslike manner. "Long distance calling."

"Speaking," Jean answered, puzzled at who would be calling during the middle of the day.

"Jean, this is Sue Watkins at Chamberland Hospital. I don't want to alarm you, but your husband Jim was just brought to the emergency room following an accident at the sawmill."

Jean gasped. "Is he all right?"

"He's resting comfortably now, but he has three broken ribs and a broken sternum and will need to be hospitalized for several days," Sue went on to explain.

Jean grabbed the counter for support. Her face turned ashen as she listened, her mind in a spin. "Tell Jim that

I'll be there as soon as possible. I'll call before I leave. Thanks for letting me know."

Jean nearly dropped the receiver as her mother entered the kitchen.

"What happened, dear? You look awful."

"Jim was injured at the sawmill. He'll be in the hospital for a few days. I wish I could go right away but the bus doesn't leave until morning."

Edith stood in stunned silence. Her heart raced. "How bad was he hurt?"

"They said he had three broken ribs and a broken sternum." Jean's voice quivered.

"I'll call Roy and see if he can drive you home. Rush upstairs and get your things packed. I'll take care of the rest."

"But Mother, I hate to leave you," Jean protested, torn between her loyalty to the two people who were the dearest to her. "I wish I could be in both places at the same time."

"Don't worry about me. Your husband needs you now. I'll be able to work something out. The Lord has never left me stranded."

Jean rushed upstairs as Edith hurriedly dialed Roy's familiar number. She briefly explained Jean's situation and he immediately put her mind to rest. "Edith, give me about a half-hour to pack a few things and gas up the car and I'll be right over to get Jean. If we leave Rocky Bluff by one-thirty she can be at the hospital in Chamberland by midnight."

"Roy, I don't know what we would do without you. You're always available to help whenever we have a crisis."

"Don't you think it's the least I could do for my future family?" he asked lightly, hoping to help her relax. "Your time is my time."

"Aren't you rushing me a little?" Edith teased, thankful for his note of levity to help break the tension she was feeling. "Remember, I haven't given you an answer yet."

"Just tell Jean I'll be there in a half-hour. We'll have everything under control and you won't have to worry about a thing." Roy's confident tone belied his growing concern that this minor crisis might be enough to upset Edith and cause another heart attack. The doctor had warned her to avoid as much stress as possible.

Edith eased herself into her reclining chair, her heart pounding wildly. She achieved a temporary calm by taking deep breaths, but it was interrupted by the buzz of the doorbell. Edith sighed and then slowly rose to answer it.

"Pastor Rhodes," Edith motioned for him to come in. "I forgot about your coming this afternoon amid all the confusion of the last few minutes. Please sit down and I'll get you a cup of coffee."

"I've had my limit of coffee for the day, but thanks for the offer." Pastor Rhodes gently guided her back to her reclining chair. "Edith, your face looks flushed. Maybe you'd better sit and rest. What can I do to help?"

"Jean just received word that Jim has been injured at the sawmill and she's upstairs packing now. Roy is driving her back to Idaho. He'll be here in a few minutes," Edith explained wearily, leaning her head back on the chair.

Pastor Rhodes sat down on the sofa. "With your

daughter gone you'll need someone to help you with the housework."

"You're right. I'm able to take care of my personal needs now, but I'm still not strong enough to do much cooking and cleaning, or the shopping."

"I'll try to find someone for you."

Jean had overheard snippets of their conversation as she entered the living room. "Pastor Rhodes, I can't thank you enough! What a load off my mind that would be, now that I'm on my way back to Chamberland," Jean said approvingly. She looked at her mother's weary face and shared a knowing look with the sensitive clergyman.

eleven

Each afternoon Roy joined Edith for her daily walks, encouraging her to go a few yards farther than she did the day before and sharing items of interest from his own life. "Edith, I was finally accepted into the Thursday morning golf mixed foursome at the country club," he told her one day. "Sounds silly to say, but I've waited a long while for such an honor."

"That's quite an exclusive circle of folks. Who did they pair you up with?"

"A woman named Sally Pegram. I've never met her, but they say she's one of the leading women golfers in the city."

"I remember Sally," Edith recalled thoughtfully. "George and I played a few rounds with her once, and she beat us soundly."

"Well, I'll need a good partner to make up for my lack of ability."

Roy reported to the clubhouse at nine-forty-five the next morning. When he checked the schedule he found that he and Sally along with Sam and Beth Porter were the third foursome to tee off. Across the room he caught a glimpse of his old friend Sam and hurried to join him and his wife. "Well, hello, Sam, Beth. It's been a long time since we've played in the same foursome. I don't think we've been together since last year's Labor Day tournament."

"Roy Dutton! What a pleasant surprise," Sam exclaimed as he extended his right hand. "Aren't you the lucky one to have Sally Pegram as a partner? I don't think there's much chance of beating that partnership."

"She'll have to play doubly well to make up for me."

Sam lowered his voice to just above a whisper. "Not only did you luck out with one of the city's best golfers, but you also got one of the nicest looking single women around."

"I've never met her but I have seen her picture in the sports pages," Roy explained. The teasing tone in Sam's voice was a little unsettling.

"The only problem with Sally is that she's desperate for a husband. I get the feeling that she's afraid of growing old alone. She might find one if she weren't so assertive around men, married or single."

"Sally couldn't be as bad as all that," Roy said, laughing. "At least I've found the woman I want to grow old with, but I'm having trouble convincing her of that fact."

"It's only a matter of time and persuasion before Edith comes around to your way of thinking," Beth observed good-naturedly.

Sally Pegram knew how to make an entrance. Wearing a bright blue knit top and light blue walking shorts that complemented her eyes and tanned body, she discreetly acknowledged the approving looks. "Hi, everybody," she greeted breezily. "I hope I didn't keep you waiting, but the traffic was terrible. There was an accident at the corner of Central and Sixth Street and only one lane of traffic for blocks."

Sally's gaze lingered leisurely on Roy and made him

uncomfortable. Suddenly she turned back to Sam. "Aren't you even going to introduce me to my partner?"

"Oh, I'm sorry," he replied, sensing Roy's embarrassment. "Sally Pegram, I'd like you to meet Roy Dutton. Roy is the director of the Crisis Center."

"How do you do, Roy?" she smiled, reaching out to shake his hand. "I did hear there was a handsome widower working there. It must be awfully exciting trying to help all those troubled young people."

Unconsciously Roy stepped backward to give himself more space as he extended his hand. "Sometimes it seems overwhelming to think that a person's life might depend on what I say." He took a deep breath and sighed. "I suppose it would be even worse if I didn't try to help at all."

To divert attention from himself, Roy checked the green on the first hole. It was clear. "Looks like the others are far enough ahead that we can get started. Is Beth going to show us how to do it?"

They strolled companionably toward the first tee. For most of the game the foursome was evenly matched except for Sally, who always seemed to take at least one less stroke per hole. The talk remained strictly on golf until they reached the twelfth green. Casually Sally turned to Roy as the Porters walked on ahead. "I would have thought you'd have remarried years ago. It must have been very difficult living alone."

"It was at times, but I think I managed quite well. I raised a son by myself and am very proud of that boy. There are too many things happening in Rocky Bluff to become bored."

When they reached the thirteenth fairway Roy was the first to tee off. After his slice to the left, Sally placed her tee in the ground and took her best driver from her golf bag. As she swung Roy admired her athletic but feminine form and tremendous power. After several weeks of nursing Edith back to health, Roy felt invigorated sharing female companionship with someone who was physically active.

They placed third in their flight that day and made plans for the tournament the following Thursday. As Roy drove home he again found himself wondering if Edith would ever have the strength to join him on the golf course. The physical exercise had revitalized his spirits and helped relieve the pent-up tension of the last few weeks.

That afternoon Roy busied himself at the Crisis Center. He had completed the installation of the sheetrock the day before and wanted to prepare the room for painting. The work was slow and tiring, but the mental picture of a comfortable, functional counseling area spurred him on. His mind drifted back to the hours he had spent with Edith in this room, helping to give her the confidence to counsel over the phone. She always seemed to say the right words in almost any situation, he mused.

Around seven o'clock Roy stopped in front of Edith's home and hurried up the front steps. As she opened the door with a friendly greeting, he gave her a quick kiss on the lips before he spoke. "It's a beautiful evening and I need a beautiful woman to share it with. Would you join me for a ride in the mountains? The fresh air will do you good."

"I've been a little down today, maybe a change of scenery will be good for me," Edith replied as she reached into the front closet for a sweater. "I'm anxious to hear about your golf game. I often considered taking up the game again after retirement." A note of resignation lingered in her voice. "I guess those days are gone forever."

The weeks of illness were beginning to pull Edith into a mild state of depression. Her strong determination, coupled with her faith of a lifetime, would not let her succumb to the discouragement for more than a few hours at a time.

As the pair turned off the main highway onto a narrow mountain road, Edith broke a long silence. "Is Sally Pegram as good as the sports writers claim?"

Roy smiled as the image of that feminine yet powerful form flashed before him. "Yes, she's good all right, but I think that the paper has overplayed her abilities. She's still human like the rest of us. What amazes me is how a woman that small can drive the ball with so much power. She can outdistance me by several yards."

"Never underestimate the power of a woman," Edith teased as they jostled over the twisting road. "Will you be playing with the same foursome next week or with different partners?"

"They have the foursomes set for the entire season so I'll be playing with Sally for at least six more weeks. Except for the fact that our skills were a total mismatch, we had a delightful time being paired with the Porters. They have a great sense of humor and keep the game lively."

Roy's eyes drifted across the horizon. The setting

sun formed a picturesque landscape of bright pinks and oranges against the tree-lined mountaintops.

Roy cleared his voice and glanced at Edith from the corner of his eye. "Now that you're feeling better do you think you'll be able to spend a few evenings a week at the Crisis Center? It would help break up your long evenings."

Tears glistened in Edith's eyes. "I'd like that very much, but I haven't felt strong enough to drive my own car yet. I'd hate to have to depend on others for transportation."

"There's always another way to accomplish the same goal," Roy persisted gently. "Would you be willing to have an extension phone installed in your house? I hate to have all of your newly acquired training go to waste."

"You do have a tremendous power of persuasion. After all that you have done for me, a few hours on the crisis phone is the least I can do."

"Good! I'll contact the phone company and see how soon they can install it. You can disconnect it any time you wish."

The following afternoon Roy joined Edith on the sofa. He wrapped his right arm around her and he pulled her next to him. "Honey, I asked you a question several weeks ago and I intend to keep on asking it. Are you ready to set a wedding date? Your health is improving daily, maybe not as fast as you'd like, but you are improving."

"Roy, I want to say yes in the worst way, but I don't think it would be fair to you. I'm not even able to do all my own housework yet, much less be an asset to a husband." She appeared cool in an ice-blue blouse that camouflaged her pounding heart.

"I've been keeping house for nearly twenty years so I'm used to all kinds of domestic chores," Roy assured her. "It would be a pleasure to serve someone who likes to eat my cooking."

They sat in silence for several moments before Roy continued. "The greatest asset to me would be someone with whom I could share my love and life."

Roy's steel-blue eyes and silver-gray hair made it difficult for Edith to remember her objections. Yet not being able to fulfill the normal duties of a housewife discouraged her. "All the same, Roy, I appreciate your offer but I don't want to be a burden on anyone. You have done so much for me already and I haven't been able to reciprocate. Ask me again when I'm able to maintain my own home."

Roy pulled her even closer. "I've told you before, Edith, that I want to marry you because of who you are, not what you can do. Take a few more days to consider."

Tears gathered in her eyes. "Maybe I just need time to get used to the idea. If you only knew how badly I want to say yes," Edith whispered softly as she laid her head upon his shoulder.

The next few days Roy busied himself with carpentry work at the Crisis Center and Edith began sewing a formal dress for Beverly Short to help pass the time. As the garment began to take shape her self-confidence was gradually restored: She was finally able to be of service to someone else. Beverly had refused payment for her help in painting the house so this was one way

Edith could show her appreciation.

When the formal was completed three days before the reception for Bev's granddaughter, Edith invited her over for a fitting. As Bev slipped into the dress and returned to the living room to model it, Edith felt satisfied.

"With work like this you can never say you're handicapped again," Bev teased as she stepped onto the stool so Edith could measure the hem. "You could become a professional seamstress."

"Flattery will get you everywhere," Edith teased lightheartedly. "As long as I can do it sitting down I'm okay. It's the physical exertion that does me in."

Normally Bob did not visit his mother unless he was bringing the children over, but for the next several days he stopped nearly every night. After the third evening Edith noticed that he disappeared into the other rooms with a tape measure and a sheet of paper. When he reappeared Edith confronted him. "Bob, I appreciate your stopping by each evening to visit. I've seen more of you this past week than I have for the last six months, but I have a feeling that something else is going on."

"Well, to be honest, there has been," he mumbled, stretching out on the sofa and putting his feet on the ottoman. "I've been visiting with Walton Realty Company and have given them the size and description of this house. They value it at $115,000 on the current market."

"Why have you been wasting your time with all that? I have no intentions of selling."

"I was just looking out for your well-being and future. Since you're not able to take care of yourself anymore it might be wiser to sell the house and move into a nursing home. Your insurance plus Medicare should be enough to keep you comfortably in the finest home in the state for the rest of your days."

Edith glared at her son, anger and frustration written on her face.

Ignoring his mother's obvious rage, Bob continued. "If the house is sold and you invest the money wisely there will be a steady income that would serve as a family legacy."

"I'm not ready to part with this house," Edith said sharply. "Your father wanted to keep this house in the family as long as possible. There are too many memories here."

"Then Nancy and I could sell our house and move into this one. We could always use the extra space. We could put our house on the market. Would you like to come with me tomorrow and talk with Richard Walton about the possibilities?"

Edith's eyes blazed with indignation. "How dare you become involved in my personal finances! I will do nothing of the sort. I'll sell this house when I feel good and ready and not a day before."

"Mother, don't get upset. I was only trying to help. Why don't you think about it for several days and then we can talk about it?"

"There is nothing to talk about, Bob," Edith retorted. "I will handle my own personal business affairs."

His face flushed with anger, he walked stiffly to the front door. "I'll be seeing you later. I have a lot of work to finish at the store tonight. Do try to relax and not let your blood pressure get too high. You know how dangerous that is for you."

With that Bob disappeared down the front steps as Edith remained in her lounge chair shaking her head. *If only Bob would understand my situation and help me instead of making life so complicated. I know I've tried to talk to him about his attitude toward money, but then so have his wife and sister and we've all failed. Only God can change him now.*

As Edith was leisurely finishing her evening meal that night, the ringing of her personal phone jerked her to attention. She reached for the receiver. "Hello, Mom. How are you?"

"Jean, it's good to hear your voice. I'm doing okay, but I'm still a little slow on my feet. How are you doing?"

"I'm doing great and Jim is almost healed from the mill accident. We thought we'd drive to Rocky Bluff for the Fourth of July weekend. Are you planning to go to the annual church picnic?"

"I sure would like to but I don't think I'll be strong enough. Beverly Short offered to take me but her family will be here and I don't want to take her away from them."

"Then we'll take you," Jean offered enthusiastically. "Would you call Bob and Nancy and make sure they'll be at the picnic? We'll make it a big family outing."

"Bob has been talking about working that day, but if he knows both you and Jim will be there maybe he'll be able to make some time to join us. I'll talk to them and let you know. Thanks for the offer."

The two chatted for a few more minutes before saying good night. Edith doubted if Bob would go to the picnic after their heated exchange of this evening but she would at least invite him. *The best way to get him to come is to first ask Nancy,* she thought. *Somehow she's generally able to remind him of his family responsibilities. I know the children will want to come if they know their Aunt Jean and Uncle Jim will be there.*

The day of the picnic the Harkness clan brought a lawn chaise for Edith and gathered around a picnic table at the fringe of the group. Everyone was anxious to talk with Jim and hear more about his accident and the plans for their new baby. After an hour of small talk and heaping portions of summer salads and grilled fare, Edith began to get drowsy. Her eyes closed.

"Jean, look at her," Bob said as he motioned to his mother. "She's getting too old to come to functions like this."

"Bob, she's just taking a little cat nap," his sister responded with disgust. "What's so unusual about that?"

"Well, nothing, except she is no longer able to take care of herself. She has to have someone come in every day and help her. That house is much too big for her to manage and yet she refuses to consider selling it."

"Why should she?" Jim spoke up sharply. "It's been her home for over thirty-five years. I think she's still able to make her own decisions."

"Mother is not being realistic about her future. She should be in a nursing home where there is someone around all the time to help look after her," Bob persisted.

"People who are much more handicapped than

Mother still enjoy independent living, why shouldn't she? Why are you so anxious to get rid of her?"

"I'm not trying to get rid of her," Bob insisted angrily. "I just think she deserves a rest."

"I want Grandma to keep her house," Jay injected. "I like that house. Dawn and I have a lot of fun there."

"I agree with you," Jean and Nancy spoke in unison.

"Well, it looks like you're outvoted," Nancy said in her typical moderator voice. "Everyone agrees that your mother should keep her house and do as much or as little as she is able to do. We will either do the rest or find someone who can."

Bob's eyes flashed but he said nothing. Dawn suddenly saw the line-up for the three-legged race and grabbed Jay's hand to run and join the others. Bob continued to sulk during the remainder of the picnic while the others went on to lighter subjects. Everyone overlooked the cloud that seemed to hang over the Harkness family.

twelve

One Saturday night as Edith was knitting a scarf and mittens for Jean the crisis phone rang. "Crisis Center, may I help you?"

"Nobody can help me," a young woman cried mournfully. "This entire mess is hopeless."

"Would you like to tell me about it?"

Through muffled sobs the answer came. "I . . . can't . . . stand . . . being . . . a mother." She struggled to continue. "Little Jeffy just keeps crying no matter what I would do, so I finally hit him and threw him in his crib. I didn't hurt him, but I didn't mean to be so rough with him."

"I understand how you feel," Edith responded sympathetically. "Sometimes when my children were little I felt the same way and had to struggle with myself to maintain control."

"But how did you do it?" the young woman questioned in a tight, controlled whisper.

"We find the inner strength to cope if we know where to turn." Edith paused to give the frustrated mother a chance to think, all the while wondering if she had come from a Christian home. "Has your baby had a medical check-up to determine the reason for his crying? Babies often have ear infections or sore throats and the mother can't tell whether or not they are in pain."

"I don't have any money to take him to a doctor.

Even if I did I'd be afraid to do it. The doctor'll only say that I'm a terrible mother. Then the authorities might take my baby away from me. If I didn't have little Jeffy I wouldn't have anything to live for."

Edith cleared her throat and took a deep breath. "There are special medical and social programs to help people in your situation. I'm sure we can find a solution. You don't have to tell me your name, but what can I call you during our conversation?"

"I don't mind telling you. It's Beth Slater," she whispered.

"I'm glad to talk to you, Beth. My name is Edith. It's often difficult to know how to handle a new baby when the pressures of life bear down upon you. Do you have anyone you feel comfortable talking with? Your husband or mother or a good friend?"

"I'm not married. When my boyfriend found out I was pregnant he left town. My mother wanted me to get an abortion so that none of her friends would know I was pregnant. I just couldn't kill my own baby, so I left home and moved to Rocky Bluff. I receive some government money but that isn't nearly enough to support me and Jeffy."

Edith thought back to the years when her own children were babies. In modern parlance, she had had the support system of a husband, two grandparents, and scores of relatives and friends to teach her about motherhood. "Learning to be a good mother doesn't always happen automatically. Have you taken any classes or read any books on child care?"

"Well, no," Beth admitted hesitantly. "I'm nursing the baby and changing his diapers. That's about all I really know how to do. Babies are supposed to have shots, but I don't know when or what kind. I think I should start him on baby food pretty soon, but I don't know when or how much."

"I'm glad you called the center, it took a lot of courage. Would you let me make an appointment with a pediatrician for you? He or she will be able tell you about shots and exactly how and what to feed Jeffy. There is nothing to be afraid of. Doctors want to help mothers and their babies, not separate them."

"Will you promise me that you won't let them take my baby away from me?"

"I promise you that as long as a child is loved and well cared for, no one will separate him from his mother. I can tell by how you talk that you love Jeffy and want the very best for him."

"I do," Beth replied with a little more confidence in her voice. "I'd do anything for him, but I don't know what to do."

"I'll call you tomorrow after I've made an appointment for you. I'll also have someone give you a ride to the doctor and home again. In the meantime, the welfare department has many services available to help new mothers. Why don't you contact the social worker who oversees your ADC claim?"

"I don't tell her anything that she doesn't ask me," Beth replied bitterly. "I'm afraid she'll put Jeffy in a foster home. She thinks a sixteen year old shouldn't have a baby. I know she does."

"Beth, social workers are trained to help people who cannot help themselves. I'm sure she has worked with many other girls with similar problems. Would you trust me to talk to her for you?"

"Well, err, I suppose. I guess I'll have to trust someone. I sure am making a mess of things myself."

Later that day Edith contacted the doctor and the welfare department. An appointment was made for the following Tuesday afternoon, and the social worker promised to make an immediate home visit to Beth and explain the training programs and educational opportunities available to young mothers.

That evening Edith dialed the girl's number. "Hello, Beth," she said to the young voice that answered the phone. "This is Edith from the Crisis Center. How are things going for you now?"

"Hi, Edith. Things are a lot better now. When Jeffy woke from his nap he was so much fun to play with. Then my social worker came to see me. She was so nice. She told me about child care classes at the community center and home study programs that will help me get my high school diploma. She left a lot of material for me to read. She said she'd come back again next week to see what I've decided to do. Thanks for calling her for me."

"I'm so glad things are going better for you. I've called the pediatrician and made an appointment for Jeffy Tuesday afternoon at two-thirty. I also arranged for one of the women from the church to provide a ride for you. Her name is Grace Blair. She'll be by at two-ten to pick you up."

"I don't know how I can ever thank you, Edith," Beth said shyly.

"Just take good care of little Jeffy and give him an extra hug from me." A bond of concern began to grow between the two although they had never met.

"You know, Roy," Edith began as the two sat alone in her living room later that night. "Situations like the one with Beth make me feel the most worthwhile. All that child needs is for someone to care about her and teach her how to cope with the routine problems of life. There are many services available to people in crisis if they only knew what to expect from each agency."

"That's so true," Roy said, nodding in agreement. "Young people often consider government agencies as enemies instead of concerned, trained people who could help them. The Crisis Center serves as a liaison between a hurting person and the source of help."

For the next few days the thought of Beth and her problems were pushed to the back of Edith's mind as she coped with the antics of her grandchildren. The following Friday evening Edith again answered the crisis phone. Instantly she recognized Beth Slater's high-pitched voice.

"Well, hello, Beth. This is Edith. How are things going for you tonight?"

"I guess I'm okay," Beth confessed meekly, "but I still get lonely always being by myself. I wish that group for young mothers met more often."

"Why don't you bring Jeffy and visit me tomorrow afternoon? I'm not able to get out as much as I'd like, but I'd enjoy getting to know you better. I used to teach home ec at the high school, and I miss being around young people."

"Well, if you're sure I wouldn't be a bother. . .but I

don't have a car."

"Where do you live? Maybe it's close enough to walk."

"318 South Windham. I have a two-room basement apartment."

"That's only three blocks from me. Why don't you bundle up Jeffy and come around two o'clock? We'll make a bed on the floor for him to take his afternoon nap and then we can have a cup of hot chocolate and a nice long visit while he sleeps."

"Thanks so much. I haven't been invited to anyone's house since I've been in Rocky Bluff."

The next afternoon Beth balanced her baby on her knee as she sat at the kitchen table while Edith made hot chocolate. As the older woman put a tablespoon of the cocoa mix into each cup and added boiling water, a look of pleasure crossed her face. "Except for my grandchildren I haven't had anyone join me for hot chocolate for a long time."

"It's so kind of you to invite me. Since it's been cold I haven't been able to get out much. Fortunately there is a corner grocery store a couple blocks from my apartment. I wish I had a car and knew how to drive."

Beth's eyes suddenly became distant. "I quit school the semester before I would have taken driver's ed."

"That's something you can take through the adult education center at the vo-tech high school. Maybe when Jeffy gets a little older you can find a part-time job and begin saving for a car of your own."

"I sure would like that," Beth replied as she took a sip of her hot chocolate. After a long pause she looked across the table at Edith. "How do you make baby food? I have to figure out how to save money."

"The softer fruits and vegetables can be put in a kitchen blender and puréed at top speed. Carrots are more difficult and you may have to add a little water. If you don't have a blender, you can use a potato masher or fork. With a little practice you will discover the proper consistency."

"I don't have a blender. All I have are a couple of plates, some cups, a saucepan, and a skillet."

"You know, I think I have an extra blender. In fact, I have two of several kitchen appliances and utensils. Would you like to have them?"

"But I can't afford to pay you," Beth protested weakly.

"They are a gift to you from me. I'll sort through them later this week and maybe you could come back Saturday and I'll have my grandson help you carry them home."

Saturday morning Edith packed a large box for Beth. Shortly after lunch Jay and Dawn stopped to see their grandmother. After serving the children cookies and milk Edith turned to her grandson. "Jay, in a little while a young woman with a small baby is going to stop for this box of pots and pans and dishes. We want to visit for a while, but when it's time for her to go home would you carry the box for her? She can't carry the baby and the box at the same time."

"It's not very far, is it?" Jay asked reluctantly as he stuffed his last cookie into his mouth.

"Only three blocks."

Just then the doorbell rang and Edith hurried across the room. When she opened the door she found Beth standing there with another teenager. "Edith, this is Anita. I hope you don't mind that I invited her to come along."

"Oh, no, I always enjoy company. Come in and make yourselves at home." Reaching for the bundle in Beth's arms, Edith gently uncovered the sleeping child. "Let me lay Jeffy in the corner and we'll sit around the kitchen table so we won't disturb him."

"Edith, I met Anita a few days ago when she moved into the apartment upstairs. She came here from New York to get married. But after she got here, her boyfriend changed his mind and went to Texas to work in the oil fields. She doesn't have enough money to get back home so she's trying to find a job here. She's awfully homesick and I thought maybe you could help her."

"I can always offer a listening ear," Edith replied as she turned to Anita. The teenager's long blond hair fell loosely around her shoulders. The tension in her facial muscles made her appear years older. "Let's begin by having something hot to drink. The two of you must be frozen."

After Anita explained more about her situation Edith's face lit up. "I can't promise you anything right now, but there may be a way for you to get a bus ticket home. The Salvation Army has a special fund to help people like you. Let me call Captain Barrett at the local mission."

The afternoon flew by as the three women shared their lives, completely ignoring Jay and Dawn at work on a jigsaw puzzle in the back bedroom.

After a couple of hours Jeffy awoke and Beth and

Anita decided it was time to go. "Beth, don't forget your box of kitchen supplies," Edith reminded her as she began putting on her coat and wrapping Jeffy in his blankets. "I'll have Jay carry them home for you."

"That won't be necessary," Anita replied quickly. "I can carry them for her." Anita stooped down and picked up the box with ease.

"Thanks so much for all you've done for me," Beth said, giving Edith a quick hug.

"You're entirely welcome. I'm glad someone can use these things." Edith turned her attention to Beth's friend. "Anita, thanks for coming. Feel free to call or stop over any time you need someone to talk with. Please give me a phone number where I can contact you after I talk with the Salvation Army."

"You can get hold of me at Beth's," the young woman replied as a warm smile spread across her face. "You remind me so much of my own mother. I don't know when I'll ever get to see her again. She has to work to support my seven brothers and sisters."

As the two young women walked down the sidewalk, Edith stood in the window and watched. *What a lot of potential those two young people have,* she thought. *I hope that I can help them over the hard spots.*

That evening Bob again stopped at his mother's home. "Mother, you look tired tonight," he said as he went to the refrigerator to get a soft drink.

"I'm fine," Edith replied as she straightened her recliner into the upright position. "Beth was over this afternoon and she brought a friend with her."

"You're spending an awful lot of time with those girls," Bob admonished as he sat on the couch. "Mom, you're getting too old to still be working with teenagers. I thought you'd given that up when you quit teaching school."

"I enjoy doing it, Bob. Why do you think I would ever be too old to help people?"

"That's n-not exactly what I meant," he stammered. "But look at you. You're exhausted. You should be having people take care of you instead of you still trying to take care of others."

Edith's jaw became fixed as she glared at her son. "I'll never be too old to help people. As long as my weak heart keeps pumping I'll do whatever I can to help others." She paused as she sent up a quick prayer for inspiration. "You know, Bob, God has blessed me with a good life and I want to share it with those less fortunate as long as I can. Now is the harvest time of my life, and I'm reaping the rewards by helping others. You're still in the planting season, Bob, and I pray someday you'll understand what this means."

thirteen

"Hi, Bob, I'm back in Rocky Bluff," Pete Dutton exclaimed as he stuck his head into the backroom of Harkness Hardware where Bob was unpacking a crate of rakes.

"Hello, Pete. Pull up a chair and sit down," Bob invited as he took the last rake from the box and tossed the box into the storage bin behind him. "Can I get you a soft drink?"

"Sure," Pete replied. He surveyed the cluttered storage room while Bob reached into the cooler, handed him a Pepsi, and pulled up a chair next to him.

"How's ranch life?"

"Busy," Pete responded, trying to sound as businesslike as possible. "The machinery kept breaking down, but I was able to fix almost everything."

"I'm proud of you, Pete. You're a genius when it comes to machines." Bob reached over to pat him on the shoulder. "I'm glad you stopped bybecause I was almost ready to give you a call. What are your plans for the next few days?"

"I'm trying to find a way to keep Dad away from that woman."

"You must mean my mother," Bob replied sympathetically. "I've been trying for eight months to keep them apart. Nothing I've tried so far has worked."

"Dad's been playing golf with another woman.

143

Maybe he'll forget Edith. I don't care if he has a golfing friend, but he doesn't need a wife."

Bob smiled to himself as he continued to manipulate information from Pete. "I wish that were true. I hear Sally is out to find a husband and she's not fussy about who it is. Some men are saying your dad is playing hard to get. All he can talk about is my mother."

"But if Dad could have a healthy golf star, why would he want a sick wife? He told me that he's asked Edith to marry him."

Bob's face turned red with rage. Could his own mother be considering remarriage without consulting him? He sat in silence for several minutes before he spoke. "Pete, don't worry about a thing. I just had an idea!"

"Good. What is it?" Pete's eyes widened with anticipation.

"Would you like to ride to Great Falls with me Monday morning?"

Pete was overwhelmed at the thought of an invitation from someone as important as Bob Harkness. "Sure, it sounds like fun. What are you going to do?"

"I plan to check the nursing homes there. I want to find the best one possible for Mother. After all the years of helping others she deserves the best of care," Bob explained, wryly remembering his recent conversation with his mother.

A puzzled look spread across Pete's face. "But how can you get her to go if she doesn't want to?"

"I'll talk to her doctor. I'm sure he'll convince her that she needs constant care to protect her damaged heart." Bob's eyes shifted aimlessly around the

storeroom before they rested on Pete. "Pete, I need
you to tell the doctor the worries your dad has about
my mom's health. I don't want it to appear like it was
all my idea."

Pete became so excited he jumped up and down. "If
Edith is in Great Falls, she and Dad can't get married!
What time are we going to leave?"

"I'll pick you up at eight if you promise not to tell
your dad why we're going. Just tell him that I have
some supplies that I need to get and that I asked you to
come along to help me load the car. I'll see you bright
and early Monday morning." The conversation ended,
Bob stood and began tearing open another shipping
crate, completely ignoring the happy young man who
slipped out the back door.

Pete nearly skipped down the street toward home.
At long last Edith would be out of his father's life for
good. She would be in a nursing home where she be-
longed and his father would only have one person to
love.

That evening Roy and Pete picked up Edith and took
her to the citywide Little League championship game
at the park. As they joined Bob, Nancy, and Dawn in
the grandstands, Pete was back to his friendly self. He
had no reason to hate Edith; Bob had everything under
control.

"I sure hope Jay's team wins," Pete exclaimed as he
watched the boys on the field warm up. "Which team
does he play on?"

"Jay's the pitcher for the Blue Jays," Dawn announced proudly. "I think they named the team after
him because he was so good and he likes the color blue.

That's him warming up there by first base."

Edith and Roy exchanged amused glances but did not amend Dawn's explanation.

As the game progressed Jay lived up to his sister's praise and struck out one batter after another. At his turns at bat he hit a double, a single, and drew a walk. Toward the end of the sixth inning Bob leaned over the others and caught Pete's attention. "Want to come to the refreshment stand with me, Pete?"

Pete nodded vigorously and jumped to his feet.

"Can I come with you, Daddy?" Dawn begged as she took hold of his hand. "I want to get some popcorn."

"I suppose so," Bob agreed reluctantly. "You can get your popcorn and go right back."

The men led the way to the concession while Dawn tagged along a few paces behind. Not realizing that she was listening, Bob put his hand on Pete's shoulder. "Are you ready to go with me Monday? I'm going to need you to convince your dad how necessary the doctor said it was for Mother to have constant care."

"That won't be hard," Pete stated proudly. "My dad always listens to what I have to say."

"Good. I don't want to waste any time. Mother will be so much better off in a nursing home in Great Falls where she can be cared for constantly."

"We are only doing what is best for her," Pete said, trying to convince himself that what he was doing was right.

"Remember, I don't want anyone to know our plans until we have the arrangements made. If your dad or my mother finds out, our entire plan will be ruined,"

Bob explained, again ignoring Dawn behind them.

"I promise not to tell a single person," Pete agreed. A depth of serious determination penetrated his voice. "At least she'll be a long ways away from my father."

Confused and upset, Dawn's eyes suddenly filled with tears. *Why don't they want Grandma in Rocky Bluff? Why are they taking her to a nursing home in Great Falls? I don't want her to leave us. I missed her so much when she was in the hospital.* She turned and started to run back to the bleachers. She must not leave her grandma, not now at least.

As Bob turned to Dawn to take her order, he caught sight of her bright red playsuit running toward the spectators. Bob shrugged his shoulders and dug in his back pocket for his wallet to pay for the snacks.

Pushing her way through the crowds, Dawn slipped in beside her grandmother and wrapped her small arms around her.

"What's wrong, honey?" Edith asked as the little girl tried to hold back her sobs.

"Nothing," she lied, burying her face in her grandmother's chest. "I just want to be with you and watch Jay play ball."

Within a few minutes Bob and Pete returned with their popcorn and drinks. Bob turned to his daughter, now leaning against his mother. "I brought you a bag of popcorn and a drink. I figured when you saw ours you'd want some too."

"Thanks, Dad," she mumbled as she shoved a handful of popcorn into her mouth and offered some to her grandmother.

When the game had ended with a victory for the

Blue Jays, 5 to 3, Jay beamed with excitement as he and his team walked across the field to receive their trophy. The Harkness and Dutton families were on their feet with the others to cheer them. Dawn pushed her fears to the back of her mind as she joined the celebration. Victory meant ice cream sundaes for everyone!

Monday morning Bob was busy at the store and didn't arrive at the Dutton home until nine. Pete hurried to the curb as soon as the familiar sedan appeared around the corner. After exchanging quick pleasantries the pair was on their way to Great Falls.

"Your mother sure looked old at the ball game. She's way too old to live alone, and way too old to marry my father!"

"I'm sure the doctor will agree with us. Besides, the nursing home will have so many social activities, it won't be long and she'll forget about your father. She's always liked to be around people," Bob assured him with pride in his ingenious scheme.

As soon as he was at the city limits Bob pressed down on the accelerator. Pete's face became ashen and he clutched the dashboard so tightly his knuckles turned white. "Aren't you going over sixty-five?"

"No cops patrol here this time of day," Bob rationalized as he pressed the gas pedal still closer to the floor. "Besides, I have to make up an hour since we were late getting started. Why don't you lie back and take a nap? It'll make the miles go faster."

In spite of his fear of speed, Pete had complete confidence in the respected, dark-haired man beside him. Within minutes he laid his head against the door frame and was fast asleep. Glancing sideways and seeing Pete's lack of attention to the speedometer, Bob accelerated even more and pulled into the other lane to pass a cattle truck.

In the oncoming lane a semi-trailer truck was only 100 yards away. Choosing between a ten-foot ditch and the truck, Bob swerved toward the ditch. He wasn't fast enough. The front end of the semi slammed into the right side of the car where Pete was sleeping. There was an instant of breaking glass and grinding metal, and then deathly silence. No one moved within the battered car.

Sirens disturbed the morning calm of Rocky Bluff as the ambulance raced toward Community Hospital. Roy Dutton, busy sanding the door frame at the Crisis Center, recalled Pete's new attitude toward Edith and him at Jay's baseball tournament. Suddenly the crisis phone rang.

No one ever calls the Crisis Center until evening, Roy thought strangely as he reached for the receiver.

"Roy Dutton?" a businesslike voice asked on the other end of the line.

"Yes," Roy replied, wondering who would know he was working here so early in the morning.

"This is Dr. Brewer at the emergency room of Community Hospital. Your son has been in a serious car accident and was brought to the hospital. Would you meet me at the emergency room right away?"

While waiting for Roy's arrival, Dr. Brewer caught sight of Pastor Rhodes who was making his routine Monday morning hospital visits.

"Pastor Rhodes, I'm glad you're here," Dr. Brewer began as he motioned for him to follow him into an empty visitors' lounge. "Is Roy Dutton a member of your congregation?"

"Yes. Is there a problem?"

"I was hoping that you might be able to help me. His son was just brought in as a DOA from an accident twenty-five miles out of town. The driver, Bob Harkness, was injured and admitted to the west wing. I called Roy and asked him to come to the hospital. Would you stay and help him during this difficult period?"

"Certainly. Has anyone contacted Edith Harkness yet? If her son was injured I'm afraid the shock might be too hard on her weak heart."

"She's been called and told about her son, but she's not aware of Pete Dutton's death. Her housekeeper is bringing her to the hospital. I'll call the nurses' station and have them watch for her. They can tell her to meet us in the emergency room as soon as she arrives. I'd rather she learn the sad news from us than from someone else."

At that moment the automatic door to the emergency room slid open and Roy Dutton walked in. Spotting Dr. Brewer with Pastor Rhodes, a lump built in Roy's throat.

Dr. Brewer motioned for him to sit down. "Roy, I have some bad news," he began as he joined Roy on the sofa. "Bob Harkness and your son were in a car accident earlier this morning. Bob suffered three broken ribs and lacerations, but he should be fine in a few days." The doctor took a deep breath. "Your son was killed instantly."

Roy sat in stunned silence as Pastor Rhodes sat on his other side. The minister rested his hand on Roy's shoulder as Roy leaned forward and buried his head in his hands and sobbed. Leaving Pastor Rhodes alone with Roy, Dr. Brewer went to meet Edith who was walking down the long corridor to the emergency room. Her face was flushed from exertion and worry.

"Mrs. Harkness, have you seen Bob yet?" Dr. Brewer asked softly.

"I was just in his room but he was resting so I didn't stay. There was a message at the nurses' station for me to come to the emergency room. No one will tell me how Pete is."

"I'm sorry, but Pete Dutton did not survive the accident. He was killed instantly." Edith's face flushed even more and her heart pounded. "Mrs. Harkness, come over and sit down," Dr. Brewer encouraged, putting his right arm around her to help support her weight. As he led her to the waiting room she spotted Roy with his face buried in his hands and Pastor Rhodes and moved to join them.

She reached out and touched Roy's arm. Instinctively he pulled her next to him and the two clung to each other in a silence that was punctuated only by an occasional sob. After several minutes Dr. Brewer took both their hands in his. "If there is anything I can do to help please feel free to call me."

Roy took a deep breath and stood up. "I suppose I better make the funeral arrangements and begin notifying family." Pastor Rhodes offered to join him as he helped Edith to her feet.

Two hours after arriving at Community Hospital Bob regained consciousness. As his eyes began to focus he saw Nancy sitting in the chair next to the bed. Tears were flowing down her cheeks. His chest was heavy with pain and there were bandages on his left arm and face.

Instinctively Nancy became aware of his stirring and went to his side. She took his head in her hands and pressed her lips against his.

"What happened?" Bob whispered with great effort.

"You collided with a semi. You have three broken ribs and other cuts, thirty-five stitches in your arm and twenty in your face, but the doctor says you should be as good as new."

"I feel miserable," Bob moaned. "How's Pete?"

If only Pastor Rhodes were here to help her break the news, she reflected with a sigh. She continued to clutch his hand in hers. "This is very hard to say," she choked, "but Pete is dead. He was killed instantly."

Bob took a deep breath, realizing his mental anguish far outweighed the pain of his body. The final moments before the impact flashed before him with clarity. He began to cry uncontrollably.

Within minutes a nurse rushed in with a hypodermic needle filled with a clear liquid. "He needs to rest. I know he's in a great deal of pain. This should help him for a while."

Bob's sobs subsided in a few moments as he drifted into a drug-induced sleep and Nancy returned to her vigil in the chair beside his bed.

Three hours later Bob again became aware of his

pain and the sterile hospital room around him. "Nancy," he whispered, as his wife tiptoed to his bedside. "Did you say that Pete Dutton was dead?"

Nancy shuddered, afraid the truth would cause the same reaction. "Yes, Bob, I'm sorry."

"I killed him!" Bob's whisper had become a drugged shout.

"Honey, you didn't kill him," Nancy said softly, cradling his head in her hands. "It was an accident."

"No, I killed him the same as if I had taken a gun and shot him," Bob persisted. "Pete warned me that I was going too fast before he went to sleep, but I was too anxious to get to Great Falls. I shouldn't have passed the cattle truck. I killed Pete Dutton!" His hysterical cries were underscored as he pounded his fist into the mattress.

As Bob's sobs and shouts again echoed up and down the west wing, the head nurse immediately called the doctor for clearance and returned to administer another shot. Within minutes Bob was asleep again.

Nancy collapsed from emotional exhaustion into the chair beside the bed. Her husband, who had always been able to control his entire world, had been completely broken within a few short hours.

When Bob awoke again a heavy gloom hung over him and he refused to discuss the accident. When visitors came he remained cold and aloof. His previous fragile emotional state had given way to listless, mechanical behavior.

Wednesday morning he was dismissed from the hospital. As Nancy drove the car into the driveway, Jay and Dawn came running to receive their customary hugs and jostling. Bob merely pushed them aside, complaining that his chest hurt too much to hug anyone.

As the day passed one hour of mental torment seemed to blend into the next. *Bob Harkness is a killer,* he kept repeating to himself. *I killed Pete Dutton.* His thoughts were confirmed when the sheriff's deputy came to his home and charged him with speeding and imprudent driving.

Thursday afternoon nearly a hundred friends and relatives gathered at the graveside after the funeral service. Bob stood as far from the others as he could. Choosing words from Paul's letters to the Corinthians and Thessalonians, Pastor Rhodes spoke in a commanding voice that echoed across the hillside:

> *Eye hath not seen, nor ear heard, neither have entered into the heart of men, the things which God hath prepared for them that love him.*

> *For our light affliction, which is but for a moment, worketh for us a far more exceeding and eternal weight of glory.*

> *For if we believe that Jesus died and rose again, even so them also that are fallen asleep in Jesus will God bring with him.*

"Pete, even if I did kill you, you are with God today," Bob whispered as if he were standing beside him instead of lying in the coffin about to be lowered into the ground.

Suddenly Bob felt a firm hand on his shoulder and he was brought back to reality. "How's it going, Bob?" Pastor Rhodes asked as the mourners began to file back to their cars.

"I don't know," he confessed sadly. "I used to have my entire world under control and now it has disintegrated into a million useless pieces. I don't know where to turn, what to do. How can I face the people of Rocky Bluff after what I have done? How can I face my own family? How can I face God?"

Wisely Pastor Rhodes momentarily ignored his questions and suggested an alternative. "Come. Let's talk in my study." Bob rode back to the church without saying a word. After the two men were seated in the minister's study, Pastor Rhodes said, "I know you lost a friend, but is there something more that is troubling you?"

Bob stared at the floor and his eyes settled on an ant as it scurried across the room. His first instinct would have been to step on it, but not today. Finally he blurted out, "I killed Pete Dutton."

The minister tried to hide his shock. "Wasn't it an accident, Bob? Did you intentionally hit that truck?"

"No, I didn't plan for it to happen, but I was driving too fast and I didn't watch what I was doing. I shouldn't even have been going to Great Falls in the first place."

"Roy told me that Pete said you were going after supplies. Was there another reason for your trip?"

Bob stammered. "I-I-I was going to find a good nursing home for Mother and then talk with the doctor and work up a legal form for her admittance. I only had selfish motives that were not in the best interest of my mother."

Pastor Rhodes watched the private battle raging inside Bob. Finally words began to tumble from Bob's mouth as if a dam had broken. "My reasons for the trip weren't at all Christian, and I took advantage of Pete's simple trust in me. I'm the one who puts on a big Christian businessman's facade, but that's all it is. Attending church is always good for business in a small city like Rocky Bluff. I've made my best contacts there. While you were speaking at the graveside I realized I really didn't know what Christianity was about. All I have been thinking about lately was how to get total control of the family business. My entire life has been centered on making money, despite the cost to anyone else."

"Bob, it's never too late to turn your life around and get into a right relationship with God. In spite of everything, your family still loves you and, most importantly, God still loves you." Pastor Rhodes took his large black study Bible from his desk and handed it to Bob. "Would you read First John, chapter one, verse nine for me?"

Bob thumbed through the New Testament hoping to stumble across the tiny book. He might be a whiz in the business world, but he was a biblical illiterate. After several minutes of searching, he began to read aloud: "If we confess our sins, he is faithful and just to forgive us our sins, and to cleanse us from all unrighteousness."

A light bulb seemed to go on within Bob's mind. The

fragmented pieces of his Christian upbringing were beginning to fall into place: He could be forgiven. As long as there is life, there is hope for changes and new beginnings. "Maybe someday God will forgive me for what I have done," he muttered.

"God forgives sins whenever we confess them, but we also have to forgive ourselves," Pastor Rhodes challenged kindly. "I realize it has been a difficult day for you. Why don't you think about God's forgiveness and the meaning of the Christian faith for a few days? I'll give you a list of Scriptures to study. We can meet again next week after you've had time to rest and seriously consider them."

"Thank you," Bob replied as he rose to leave. "Money almost became my god. It has nearly destroyed my life and the lives of those I've loved the most. There has to be a better way to live and I'm determined to find it."

The next few days Bob spent many hours resting in bed. When he was not sleeping he was studying his Bible and thinking. *Why have I been so inconsiderate and uncaring toward Mother? She taught me the right way to live and I refused to listen. Because of that I indirectly caused Pete's death. There will never be a time that Mother will be too old to know what is right and wrong. Her body may be slowing down, but her loving spirit will always be young and alive.*

Bob paused. *A special peace surrounded him. If Jesus could forgive the thief on the cross, surely He can forgive me.* Bob questioned himself and his motives for some time. In the end, there was no booming voice or flashing lights but in that afternoon stillness the same

Savior who had been a constant companion and friend of his mother became a reality to Bob Harkness. A serenity filled his troubled mind as he thought of ways he could show his mother his gratefulness for all she had done for him.

First, however, he had to face Roy Dutton.

fourteen

The morning after Pete's funeral Roy awoke with a dull headache. As he lay in bed trying without success to go back to sleep, he came to a stark conclusion. The world of grief and sudden loss was his to face alone. After an hour of staring blankly at the ceiling he stumbled out of bed. He paused at the closed door to Pete's room and then hesitantly opened it. Waves of happy memories washed over him. *Why did that senseless accident have to happen?* he asked himself. *Pete led a life of simple innocence, why did it have to end this way?*

After a Spartan breakfast of cold cereal and black coffee, Roy dressed in an old plaid shirt and faded blue jeans and headed for the Crisis Center. "Good morning, Roy," Dan Blair, one of the volunteers, greeted as Roy strolled into the center with an emotionless expression on his face. "I'm sorry to hear about the loss of your son. I thought you might like some help with the painting."

"Thanks, Dan," Roy responded, sinking into the padded chair by the door. "I don't know what I'd have done without you taking over the switchboards and organizing the volunteers for me. With so many things on my mind this week I'm afraid I abandoned the Crisis Center."

"That's understandable. I enjoy helping. Our union

went on strike last week and I don't know when we'll be called back to work. Most of the other bus drivers are spending their time walking the picket line but I'm not the militant type. I'd rather be working at something. I suppose I might feel differently about the strike if I had a wife and children to support."

"I'll be able to put you to good use here, if you have the extra time," Roy replied as he picked up a paint roller and began spreading light blue paint on the west wall. "I can finish the manual labor, but I'm not ready to deal with other people's problems. Dan, would you mind taking over for me until you're called back to work?"

"Not in the least. Just let me know what needs to be done and I'll see that it gets done."

The two men finished painting the room in less than two hours. Few words were spoken between them, but Dan's presence was a comfort to Roy. Before leaving Roy took out a sheet of paper and briefly outlined the procedures of the Crisis Center and the personnel involved. As he handed it to Dan he breathed a sigh of relief. The work of the center could go on without him.

On the way home Roy decided to stop at Bea's for a bite to eat. As he gazed idly through the side window, Sally Pegram approached his booth and silently slid into the seat across from him.

"I'm sorry to hear about your son," she began as she took his hand in hers. "If there's anything I can do please let me know."

Roy's eyes met hers, but the feeling of despondency remained. "There's not much anyone can do right now. I guess I just need time to help fill the void."

"How about a game of golf in the morning? We were such good partners during the mixed foursome tournament, I'd hate to let our talents go to waste."

"Sally, I'm having trouble getting interested in anything at this point."

"You need to force yourself to do something. The fresh air and crisp September wind will be good for you. Playing golf always lifts my spirits and gets my mind off my troubles."

"It might be worth a try. I can't keep my mind on anything else, but I warn you that I'm pretty lousy company right now."

"I'll take my chances," Sally said lightly as she stood to leave. "I'll meet you at the clubhouse at ten."

Roy watched her as she strolled gracefully out of the restaurant. *Maybe she's right. A change of pace might be good for me. I do need some good old-fashioned relaxation.*

The next morning as they approached the green of the seventh hole, Sally had endured enough of Roy's sullen silence. "I know it hurts deeply that Pete died, but don't take it so hard," she said nonchalantly. "Maybe it was for the best anyway. After all, he was mentally retarded, and who would have taken care of him if you died first?"

Sally's words cut through Roy like a surgeon's scalpel. *Surely she doesn't realize what she is saying,* he tried to rationalize. *Maybe she's one who stumbles over words in a tight situation.* After a long pause Roy answered, "The Davidsons would have always provided a home and job for him. Even if he were retarded he could have been an excellent mechanic for any rancher or farmer." His speech was slow and deliberate and his face reddened with anger.

"I didn't mean to upset you," Sally replied in a sugary sweet voice as she took her putter out of her golf bag. "But this way Pete will never be a drain on society. He's happier where he is now."

"Pete had more love and compassion than most of the leaders in our community. He was an asset to society, not a detriment," Roy snapped. "I can't imagine anyone thinking otherwise." With that he approached the eighth tee-off area. He firmly pushed his tee into the ground, placed the ball on it, and with one powerful swing sent the ball farther than he ever had in his life.

"I'm sorry," Sally said quietly, while pouting as Roy placed his driver back into his bag. "I thought maybe I could help you see things more realistically."

The pair finished the ninth hole in silence and Roy hurried to his car, scarcely saying goodbye. Sally tagged behind him with a puzzled look on her face. "Do you think we could get together for another game before the weather turns cold?"

"I think I've had enough golf for the season," Roy answered dryly as he opened his trunk and laid his clubs next to his spare tire.

Instead of heading home Roy turned down a side street and went straight to the Harkness home. The thought that somehow Edith's son may have been responsible for Pete's death had created an uneasy tension between them. He tried to shove those thoughts into the background and visualize the laughing, caring person who had been his prize student in the volunteers' class.

Edith answered the door dressed in a crisp lavender pantsuit. The worry lines that had appeared during her surgery had reappeared on her flawless skin. "I'm glad to see you," she greeted as she motioned for him to have a seat on the sofa. "I've been concerned about you. I've scarcely talked to you since we left the mortuary Monday afternoon. I called your house several times but you weren't home."

As Roy sat on the living room sofa a warmth began to replace his numbness. He marveled at Edith's compassion and depth of character that far outweighed what he had experienced with Sally. He basked in the silence of her presence before he spoke. "I finished painting the walls at the Crisis Center yesterday and then I went golfing this morning with Sally."

"The exercise should have been good for you," Edith replied taking his hand in hers.

Roy gave a sarcastic laugh. "The exercise was great, but the company was devastating."

"What happened? It's not like you to talk that way about anybody."

"I've never known anyone to have such a low regard for human life, almost a Nazi-like mentality, and believe me, I cringe at that description. She would have been perfectly content in a society intent on destroying all misfits to produce a perfect race."

Edith paused, searching for the appropriate words. "I don't know exactly what she said and I'm probably better off not knowing. This is the time when our faith is put to the greatest test. You must forgive even when you heart is broken."

"I wish I could honestly say I can, but all I can say at this moment is that I'm willing for God to help me forgive. I'm not able to do that with my own strength."

"Our willingness is all He expects. If we trust God, the details will take care of themselves."

For the next hour the two shared their thoughts more deeply than they had before. All of their hurts and heartaches were exposed as their mutual love and trust blossomed. Finally Edith looked at the clock and gasped. "Roy, it's nearly one-thirty and I'll bet you haven't had any lunch."

"You're right. I was so angry I forgot all about food."

"The housekeeper fixed a large pot of chili last night before she left. How about having some with me? It's not any fun eating alone."

Roy heartily agreed and followed her to the kitchen. He began getting the bowls and silverware from the cupboard as Edith took the pot of chili from the refrigerator. They worked in peaceful silence until lunch was at last on the table and then Roy asked the blessing. As Edith filled the bowls, she began a humorous digression of Jay and Dawn's start of another school year that buoyed Roy's downcast spirits.

"Edith, why don't you go lie down and rest? I'll finish the dishes," Roy volunteered as the last bite of chili disappeared from her bowl. "I'll see you at church tomorrow."

"I've learned never to turn down an offer for help. I am getting a little tired." She gave Roy a kiss on the lips and disappeared into her bedroom as he began clearing the table. The bond between them had not been weakened because of Pete's accident, Roy realized, but any mention of the tragedy had been tactfully avoided.

The next morning Bob and Nancy and the children gave Edith a ride to church. While Bob seemed happier and more relaxed than he had in years, his behavior seemed strange to Edith after such a traumatic week. The children chattered about their new year in school. The joy in the car was in sharp contrast to the pain and heartache that Edith kept hidden within herself.

As the organist played the prelude, Roy quietly slid into the pew next to Edith. They both whispered soft hellos and then withdrew into their own thoughts. As Edith studied his sturdy, handsome face she realized she had not noticed the night before how he had aged in the last week. The laughter lines that she cherished had deepened into crevices of worry.

As the congregation sang "What a Friend We Have in Jesus, All Our Sins and Griefs to Bear," Edith again glanced at Roy and noticed a tear sliding down his cheek. *If only Roy would let Jesus carry his grief instead of trying to carry it alone,* she prayed with tears welling up in her own eyes.

As the congregation gathered in small groups on the sidewalk outside the church following the worship service, Nancy turned to Roy as he descended the front steps. "Mom is coming home with us for Sunday dinner. Why don't you join us? We'd love to have you."

Roy hesitated and gazed into the distance. "Thanks for the offer, Nancy, but could I take a rain check? I think I'd prefer to be by myself for a while. Last Sunday Pete was sitting beside me in the pew and today he's gone."

"Well, if you change your mind, please feel free to come over later," Nancy encouraged, giving his arm a gentle squeeze.

Roy was embarrassed to offer such a lie when the truth was vivid in his mind. He could not bear to face the man who was responsible for his son's death. Although everyone said it was an accident, he still needed someone to blame. After all, the accident report had stated that excessive speed was involved.

After dinner, instead of going directly to his bedroom to rest, Bob stretched out on the living room sofa. Mentally Edith kept rehearsing what she would say to Nancy and hoped that Bob would soon retire to his bed. However, none of her rehearsed words seemed suitable to the situation, and her son did not budge from the couch.

As the women joined Bob in the living room, he sat up and a flood of words poured from his mouth like a bursting dam. "Mom, I don't know how to say this, but I'm really sorry for the way I have treated you lately. I was more concerned about making money than your personal welfare."

Edith stared at him in disbelief. After a long silence she replied softly, "What brought all that on?"

"It's a long story. But as I was standing over Pete's grave I realized what an innocent trust he had in me, and, more importantly, what a simple faith he had in God. I felt pretty ashamed of myself. After the funeral I had a long talk with Pastor Rhodes and he gave me some Scripture to study. I came home and did a lot of soul searching. You know, Mom, I sat beside you in church every Sunday for many years and I don't think I ever listened to a word that was said until I had made such a mess out of my life that I didn't know how to get out of it. Only when I was at the end of my rope did I turn to God for help. I can honestly say that from now on I'm going to follow Christ, whatever the cost, even if it means I have to give up the business."

Edith could not contain her excitement. She had been waiting for years to hear those words. "I'm so happy for you," she said as she gave him a hug. "My deepest prayer has been that my entire family would surrender their lives to Christ before I die."

"There's one other thing I need to say," Bob continued as he lowered his gaze, afraid to make eye contact with his mother. "I think you ought to keep the house as long as you can. I can help you with the regular maintenance and Nancy said she'd help with the inside work. To be honest, I only wanted you to sell so that I could protect my personal inheritance. That's how ugly I had become. Please forgive me. I'll try to make it up to you any way I can."

Tears filled Edith's eyes at Bob's honest confession. The integrity he had been taught by his father was finally beginning to show. "I knew all along that was what you were trying to do and that's why I refused to sell. Let's put all the hard feelings behind us. I came over today to talk to Nancy about helping me with the housework until I can find a buyer. *I* have decided to sell the house."

"But Mother, are you sure you want to sell?" Bob questioned softly. "Don't let anyone influence you one way or the other. We know how much your home has meant to you throughout the years. Remember all the good times you've enjoyed in that house. You shouldn't make such an important decision on the spur of the moment."

Edith's eyes roamed idly out the picture window. The leaves on the willow trees were turning a golden brown. Another season was beginning. "I have to be realistic about my physical limitations and accept the fact that my house is too big for one person. I probably could find a small, one-bedroom apartment that would fit my needs much better."

"If you're certain that's what you want, I'll be willing to help you," Bob offered cautiously. He paused for a few moments, deep in thought. "I'd feel better if you set up your assets to go to your favorite charity. That way I can prove to you that I'm interested in you and not the family inheritance."

Edith studied her son. The change in him between Thursday and Sunday was unbelievable. Yet underneath his brazen exterior she had always sensed the gentle, compassionate spirit that had now surfaced.

"Bob, I do want your help. Now maybe I can begin to put some trust in your judgment and financial advice. I'm proud of you. It takes a pretty big man to admit his shortcomings. I feel that a new era in our relationship is before us."

fifteen

The following Monday Roy drove Edith to Great Falls for a follow-up visit with her cardiologist. The news was worse than expected. Edith's heart had suffered permanent damage and she would have to limit her activities.

Upon returning home Edith had just unlocked the back door and invited Roy inside when the phone rang. "Hello, Grandma." Dawn's words were punctuated by muffled sobs. "You did come home after all. Can I come and see you?"

"Well, certainly, honey, if it's all right with your mother. But why are you crying?"

"I just want to see you," Dawn managed through her gasping cries. There was a momentary silence while the weeping child raced to find her mother. "Mommy said I could come so long as I am home by bedtime. I'll ride my new bicycle and be there in a few minutes."

Edith hung up the phone and turned to Roy. "That was strange. I've never heard Dawn this upset before. She acted like she didn't think I was ever coming home again. I wonder where she got that idea?"

"Children have a way of misinterpreting things. I'm sure that it's nothing serious."

When Edith opened the front door to greet her granddaughter, Dawn wrapped her arms around her waist,

buried her head on her chest, and continued to sob.
Edith led the child to the sofa and cuddled her while
Roy watched with compassion. "Why did you think
that I was never going to come home again?"

"Because you went to Great Falls. I thought Roy
was going to put you in a nursing home there and I'd
never get to see you again."

"Whatever gave you that idea? I merely went to see
the doctor."

"At Jay's last baseball game I heard Daddy and Pete
talking about going to Great Falls to find a nursing home
for you. They were on their way to Great Falls when
the accident happened."

Roy's face turned red with anger as he attempted to
control himself in Dawn's presence. He remained rigid
on the living room sofa while Edith led her granddaughter to the kitchen.

Edith fixed Dawn a cup of hot chocolate and handed
her the cookie jar. "Dawn, the doctor said I'm still
strong enough to live by myself. I just won't be able to
do all the things I used to do. If I ever do need to go to
a nursing home I'll go to the one here in Rocky Bluff.
That way you will be able to come and see me every-
day."

After finishing her snack Dawn returned to her normal bubbly self. "Grandma, I'm glad you're going to
be in Rocky Bluff forever. I'm going home now to tell
Jay." With that Dawn raced out the front door, barely
managing a quick goodbye to Roy on her way.

Edith turned to Roy. "I'm sorry you had to hear the
reason for Bob's trip this way. I didn't learn about it
until the other day and I didn't know how to tell you. I

didn't want to hurt you anymore. You've already been through so much. I was going to wait until the timing was right to tell you."

"I think the time is right, right now." Edith had never heard Roy's voice so harsh and demanding. "After all, it was my son who was killed in the accident. Why would he be a part of putting you in a nursing home?"

"Pete was jealous of our relationship. We both knew that. I'm sorry to say that it was my own son's idea for him to come along. Bob took full advantage of Pete's innocent trust."

"How can you forgive him for such a thing and pretend like nothing ever happened?" Roy demanded, pounding his fist into the arm of the chair. "While being part of this fiasco to get rid of you, he killed my son."

"Roy, I had to forgive Bob because Christ forgave me for all the selfish things that I've done. What is helping me the most is to know that God is bringing good from a tragic situation."

"What good could possibly come from Pete's death?" Roy demanded.

Edith took a deep breath as she tried to choose her words carefully. "The day of Pete's funeral Bob realized what he had done and became truly remorseful. He has had a complete change of heart and is now beginning to be less concerned about money and his own self-interests and more concerned about other people. You won't believe how different he is now."

"I'll believe it when I see it. The jails are full of people who suddenly 'get religion' after they've gotten themselves into trouble," Roy shouted. "You expect me to take it lightly that Bob could kill my son and then make it right by a simple confession of faith and begging forgiveness? I'll have to see the change before I'll believe anything."

"Spend more time with him, Roy. Then you'll see what I mean. Don't just take my word for it. Bob didn't intend for Pete to die. He wants to beg your forgiveness and to make amends for what has happened but he doesn't know how. He is carrying around a tremendous sense of guilt."

"I don't know if I can face that man again as long as I live." He paused and took a deep breath. He was torn between the woman he loved and the hatred he felt toward her son, the man who had killed, albeit accidentally, his only son.

The room seemed to fill with tension as the clock ticked loudly from the mantel. "Maybe I'd better go home now and cool off. I'll call you in the morning. Good night, Edith." With that Roy turned and stomped out the back door, slamming it behind him.

Edith took a deep breath and then checked the phone directory and dialed the Rhodes residence. In a few moments a deep voice answered. "Pastor Rhodes. May I help you?"

"Hello, Pastor, this is Edith Harkness. I hate to disturb you at home, but I have a problem that I don't know how to handle, and I thought you might be able to help."

"I'll be glad to do anything I can. What's happening?"

"Roy just found out that Bob and Pete were on their way to Great Falls to arrange to put me in a nursing home when the accident happened. I've never seen him so angry. He feels that Bob manipulated Pete and then accidentally killed him. I tried to explain that Bob has since repented and turned his life around but I felt like I was talking to a brick wall. I'm frightened for him. Is there anything you can do?"

"Don't let Roy's anger upset you. It's a very natural emotion for him at this time. Anger is one stage of the grieving process. I'll go and visit with him right away. Don't worry, I won't let on that you sent me."

Edith breathed a sigh of relief. "Thank you for your concern. I don't know how we'd get along without you during this difficult time."

"That's what I'm here for."

As Edith prepared for bed that night, she felt she carried the weight of the world on her now drooping shoulders. The doctor's diagnosis, Dawn's knowledge of the accident, and Roy's outburst of anger all contributed to her mental and physical exhaustion. As she straightened the heirloom quilt on her four-poster bed, the ringing phone made her lose her balance momentarily.

"Hello, Grandma. Congratulations!" Her son-in-law's cheerful voice greeted her.

"Well, hello, Jim. Do you have some good news for me? I need some for the day."

"I sure do. Jean had a baby girl at nine o'clock tonight. Gloria Lynn weighs eight pounds and three ounces and is the most beautiful child I've ever seen. Jean will be out of the hospital in a couple days. Will you be able to come and stay with us like we planned?"

"I'd love to, but I'm afraid I wouldn't be much help

around the house. The doctor has placed so many limitations on me."

"That's all right, Mom. I'll get the housework done, but Jean insists that it's traditional for the maternal grandmother to come and give a new mother pointers on child care. How soon will you be able to leave?"

"I suppose I could take the bus that arrives in Chamberland at eight-twenty the day after tomorrow if you'll meet me. I have several things I need to do tomorrow."

"Great! I'll meet the Friday night bus from Rocky Bluff. Just don't spoil my daughter too much. That's my job."

As Edith lay in bed that night the intensity of her life engulfed her. Never before had she felt so many conflicting emotions at the same time: the love of her family, the joy of a new grandchild, the pain of death, and the helplessness of being unable to comfort the man she loved. The doctor had been right. During her latter years she had learned what things in life were important and what things would pass away.

The next morning Edith wanted to call Roy and tell him the exciting news but she was afraid he might be sleeping late. The night before he had promised to call but the phone had been silent all morning. Early that afternoon the doorbell rang. She expected to see Roy but found her minister standing there instead. "Hello, Pastor Rhodes, do come in."

"Good afternoon. How are things going today? Were you able to get a good night's rest?"

Edith sighed as she remembered her sleepless night. "Not really. I'm extremely concerned about Roy, plus

I received word that Jean had a baby girl last night."

"Congratulations. Are you planning to go to Idaho to be with them?"

"I hope to leave on tomorrow morning's bus, but I don't really want to leave Roy. You know how despondent he's been since the accident."

"I understand why you feel that way, but I would suggest that you go ahead and be with your family. I had a long talk with Roy last night. Right now he is having trouble dealing with his own feelings about the accident but he doesn't want that to destroy your relationship. That is why he asked that I come by and talk with you."

"But what did he say?" Edith's eyes froze. The thought of losing Roy's friendship was overwhelming.

"He's afraid to see you for a few days for fear he would say something that he would later regret. I'm certain everything will work out in the end," Pastor Rhodes assured her. "Roy needs time to grieve over his dead son."

Edith's mind drifted back nearly twelve years to when she had suffered a similar loss. "I've been there myself. When George died I stayed in the house for almost three weeks before I even ventured to the store. Then I had so many conflicting feelings that I needed time by myself to sort them through. I know people had trouble understanding my need for solitude. Roy must be experiencing the same thing, but I'm concerned about him being alone."

"I assure you I'll be visiting Roy as often as possible while you're away. We must put him in the Lord's hands during this difficult time. In the end there is little either you or I can do; only God can heal a broken heart."

The first Sunday after Edith left for Chamberland, Roy stretched out in front of his TV and watched a football game. His peace was abruptly disturbed by a loud knock on the front door. Suddenly he found himself face to face with Bob Harkness.

His attitude toward Bob was beginning to soften, but he was not yet certain that they could carry on a worthwhile conversation. Almost mechanically, he invited him in and turned off the TV.

"I hope I'm not disturbing you," Bob began as he entered the living room with reluctance. "I have wanted to talk to you for some time, but I didn't have the courage."

"Please sit down and I'll get you a soft drink. Do you like yours in a can or with ice?"

"I'm not fancy. Straight from the can is fine."

In a few moments Roy returned with a drink for Bob. "Have you been following the Vikings this season?"

"I catch a game now and then. I hear they're having a pretty good season."

"That they are."

The two men sat in uncomfortable silence for a few minutes. Finally Bob cleared his throat and spoke. "This is the hardest thing I have had to do in my life. Six months ago I would never have dreamed that I would be begging someone's forgiveness. I thought I had my entire life under control. Roy, I regret that I have hurt so many people and I know I am responsible for Pete's death."

"Regrets will never bring Pete back to life," Roy replied without emotion. His body became rigid and his icy gaze froze Bob to his chair.

"How well I know. I've agonized over this ever since the accident. Although I was raised in the church with fine Christian parents, I completely missed the love and forgiveness that Christ offers."

There was a long, tense silence before Bob continued. "When I was faced with the fact that it was my own selfishness that indirectly led to Pete's death, all I could do was plead for mercy. I wish there was some way I could make up for what happened, but all I can do is beg for your forgiveness."

Roy's scowling expression caused Bob to hesitate and take a deep breath. "Also, I can't find words to tell you how much I appreciate your love and concern for my mother, especially during her long illness."

Fragments of the Lord's Prayer flashed through Roy's mind. "Forgive us our trespasses as we forgive those who trespass against us." *Can I live what I speak? Bob seems sincere. Can I turn him away when he is literally begging for my forgiveness?*

The struggles within Roy mounted. He must completely forgive Bob or become hard and bitter for the remainder of his life. After an unbearable silence Roy looked the young man straight in the eyes and whispered, "Yes, I do forgive you. I accept the change that God has made in your life."

Suddenly tears of relief filled the older man's eyes and his shoulders shook with his sobs. Washed away with these tears were his hostilities, frustration, and anger toward the man whom he'd considered responsible for his son's death.

As Bob watched him tears also filled his eyes. Words were not necessary to express the healing that was transpiring between the two men. Life could now go on without the shadow of the accident casting a pall over their relationship and Roy's relationship with Edith.

After that Sunday Roy was able at last to face the empty room in his house. At the same time he began to miss the companionship and good times he had shared with Edith. When he called her in Chamberland the next evening he learned that she would be coming home the following Wednesday. She sounded so excited about the new grandbaby and promised scores of pictures to substantiate her claim of a beautiful child.

Wednesday afternoon Roy busied himself with preparations for Edith's return. He made a pineapple upside-down cake, a tossed salad, and a large pot of spaghetti sauce. That evening Bob, Nancy, and the children joined him at the bus station. Everyone was anxious to hear about the new baby and to welcome Edith back to Rocky Bluff.

After the evening meal everyone remained around the dining room table while Roy stacked the dishes in the dishwasher and then returned to his place. They reveled in a new openness and freshness in their family love. Finally Roy, unable to contain himself, rose to his feet in a mock formal manner.

"Ladies and gentlemen, we have gathered here at this joyful occasion to make public the engagement and approaching marriage of Roy Dutton and Edith Harkness. Everyone in favor please say aye."

The children immediately shouted their approval while all heads turned toward Edith. Tears filled her eyes. "After hearing the doctor's discussion of my physical limitations are you sure you want to go through with this?"

"The doctor didn't say you were mentally limited, did he?" Roy teased as the children giggled.

"Well, of course not."

"Then this is what I want to do. We are taking a family vote. Edith Harkness, how do you vote?"

Words failed her as she stood and embraced her dearest friend. As their lips touched momentarily, Nancy and Bob clapped and shouted their ayes and laughter filled the room.

The next morning Roy awoke to a city blanketed with snow. As he peered out his frosted window, he saw a parallel between the winter scene and his life. As the stark bareness of the oak trees was now covered with a snowy comforter, so the nakedness of his anguished soul was now clothed with a new love. Edith had agreed to be his bride, and they had the full support of her family.

After breakfast Roy bundled himself up for the winter weather and walked to the Crisis Center, invigorated by the crisp morning air. As he entered the back room of the center, Dan Blair had just finished sweeping the tile floor and rearranging the throw rugs.

"Good morning, Dan."

"Roy, it's good to have you back! The calls have nearly doubled with the approach of the colder weather. I was beginning to think that we might need two volunteers on duty again to help prevent what happened last year with Susan Youngman."

"We'll call a meeting of all the volunteers and work out a schedule for the holiday season sometime next week."

"That sounds like a good idea." Dan hesitated before continuing. "My union settled their strike late last night and they are calling all bus drivers back to work Monday. Can someone else carry on?"

"Don't worry about a thing. I know it's been difficult for you and the others who have been on strike for six weeks. I appreciate all the work you've done."

The men visited for another hour concerning the events of the past few weeks. Roy felt he was again in contact with the needs of the community. It was good to be back at the center after so many weeks of only feeling his personal pain. After Dan left he stayed at his desk for another hour to catch up on the mounds of paper work.

The next afternoon Roy parked his car in Edith's driveway. Instead of going to the door he found a shovel in the garage and began clearing a path down the front sidewalk. Halfway down the walk Roy took a rest and spotted Edith standing in the picture window smiling. He waved at her and returned to scooping snow as she returned the gesture. *How can she consider herself an invalid when she has so much to offer?* he thought suddenly.

When he finished the walk Roy leaned the shovel beside the garage door and slipped into the back porch to take off his boots and shake the snow from his coat and hat. Edith greeted him with a smile. "You didn't have to do that. I could have Jay shovel the sidewalk when he gets home from school."

"It was my pleasure." Roy stepped into her warm kitchen and took off his coat. "The least you could do for a freezing old man would be to offer him a hot cup of coffee," he teased, pulling up a chair at the table.

As they sipped their coffee in silence, Roy searched for exactly the right words. "Edith, I don't want to wait any longer. We've been through so much together. Let's get married as soon as possible." He took a deep breath. "How about December thirty-first?"

At first Edith hesitated as if she had not heard what he said. Marriage to Roy seemed the natural and right thing to do. She entwined her fingers through his as her face glowed with love.

"That's fine with me, but why did you pick New Year's Eve of all times?"

"We'll only have our family and close friends at the wedding but the entire world will be celebrating with us. How's that for logic? We can start out the new year afresh with a new life together. I wonder if Pastor Rhodes will be able to perform the ceremony that night?"

"That all sounds so easy, but we have two separate homes to combine," Edith protested weakly. "I know I have been hesitant to part with this house, but why don't we just let Bob go ahead and sell it?"

"That's fine with me," Roy agreed as he took her face in his hands. "Edith, my dear, my place is plenty big enough for the both of us."

sixteen

The day after Thanksgiving the phone rang in the Harkness home as Edith was finishing the lunch dishes.

"Hello, Edith, this is Grady Walker at the school. It's been a long time since I've seen you. How have you been?"

"I'm moving slower, but I seem to be keeping busy. How are things at school?"

"We've all been involved in the new building project. If you've been by the north side of the building lately, you've probably seen that the new wing is nearly completed."

"It doesn't seem like any time at all since they had the ground-breaking ceremony."

"Why I called, Edith, is to see if you would come to the school sometime this week. There are a few things I'd like to discuss with you."

"I don't see a problem. How would tomorrow afternoon be?"

"That would be great. How about two-thirty?"

The time agreed upon, Edith hung up the phone mystified as to why Grady would want her to come to the school. Grady knew that she was no longer able to substitute teach and she had had very little contact with the school since she retired.

The next afternoon a flood of memories overwhelmed Edith as she walked into Rocky Bluff High School. The walls had been repainted and the floors shined. The faces of the students were different, but it felt like she was coming home. Viola greeted her warmly and ushered her into the principal's office. Grady was sitting at the table with Dick Ritter, chairperson of the school board.

The principal greeted her and extended his hand. "I think you know Dick Ritter."

"Oh, yes," Edith assured him as she shook hands with a long-time acquaintance. "It's good to see you again."

After a few minutes of small talk shared over coffee, Grady finally came to the point of the meeting. "I suppose you're wondering why I had you come today. Your contributions to Rocky Bluff High School have not gone unnoticed. In fact, I most likely would not be here today if it weren't for your quick actions."

"I only did what had to be done at the time," Edith insisted. "I think if I'd had time to think I would never have been brave enough to take the gun away from Larry."

"You not only saved my life, but for ten years you provided the best education and role model Rocky Bluff students could have. In recognition of your contribution to Rocky Bluff High, the school board has unanimously voted to name the new addition the Edith Harkness Wing, with your permission of course."

Edith sat speechless. Never had she thought she would receive such an honor after such a quiet, ordinary life. "But I don't deserve such an honor," she objected weakly.

"The school board believes you do. No one has consistently made as many contributions to Rocky Bluff

High School as you. If you agree, I'll make the decision public next week."

"Oh, Grady, I feel so humble at this moment. Of course, you may name the new wing after me, but I still say I don't deserve this honor."

In the days that followed Edith was overwhelmed but she could not spend time thinking about it. She was in a flurry of wedding and moving plans. Everything seemed to be happening at once.

On December thirty-first Pastor Rhodes stood before a small gathering in the intimate church chapel. As he read the timeless words pronouncing Roy and Edith husband and wife in the name of the Father, and of the Son, and of the Holy Ghost, he beamed approvingly at the couple standing before him. He had shared many joys and heartaches with them over the years as their pastor. Tonight was a milestone in their lives, and he was honored to be a part of it.

"Pastor Rhodes, you and your wife are planning to join us at the reception at Nancy and Bob's home this evening, aren't you?" Roy asked after the ceremony. "The women have been working for several weeks to provide us with a gala affair."

"I wouldn't miss it for the world. I'll be over in a few minutes after I turn down the heat and lock the building."

"Don't wait too long," Nancy teased. "You don't want to miss the cake cutting."

Among the guests who had traveled great distances to celebrate the New Year's Eve wedding were Jean and Jim with Gloria Lynn from Idaho, Roy's brother and his family from Miles City, Montana, and Edith's sister from California. When Gloria Lynn let out a big cry Jean hurriedly bundled her in the afghan that Edith had crocheted as a Christmas gift.

"It sounds like it's feeding time," the new mother sighed contentedly. "If you all don't mind, Jim and I will leave for Bob's now so I can perform my duties."

"The housekeeper is at the house now to finish setting up and welcome guests so just make yourself at home," Bob said as he walked them to their car. "We'll be along shortly."

Within a half-hour more than fifty guests were gathered in the Harkness home. Jay and Dawn were beside themselves with excitement. "Grandma, I bet I'm the only one in my room at school who got to go to their grandmother's wedding!" Dawn giggled. "I hope I can have a picture to prove to everyone that I did."

"As many pictures as your Uncle Jim has been taking, I'm sure there'll be enough for the entire town," Edith replied as she winked at her overeager photographer.

Eyeing her mother-in-law across the room, Nancy motioned her to join the group assembling around the beautifully decorated serving table. "Mom, do you and Roy want to cut the cake so we can begin serving?"

Edith took Roy's hand as she led him behind the table. Her fingers covered his as she helped guide the knife through the thick icing, cutting two small pieces.

"We have to do this properly," Jim teased. "The most important picture at the wedding is the one with the bride and groom feeding each other a piece of wedding cake." After adjusting the lens, he snapped the shutter as Roy and Edith simultaneously shoved a piece of cake into each other's mouth. Everyone cheered with delight. Edith reached for a napkin to wipe her face and fingers as Roy chuckled at the frosting on her nose.

As midnight approached, the wedding guests prepared to toast the bridal couple with the fruit punch Jean had prepared that afternoon. "To a long, happy life together," Pastor Rhodes began.

"Best wishes to the newlyweds," Bob said as he lifted his glass. His eyes misted over as he looked deep into his mother's eyes. "Mom, I want you to know you'll never be too old to enjoy life. I wish you both happiness, good health . . . and the presence of mind to throw me out the door if I should ever interfere! I love you both."

Laughter erupted in the dining room and then one by one each of the guests proposed a toast to the radiant Mr. and Mrs. Roy Dutton.

A Letter To Our Readers

Dear Reader:

In order that we might better contribute to your reading enjoyment, we would appreciate your taking a few minutes to respond to the following questions. When completed, please return to the following:

Rebecca Germany, Editor
Heartsong Presents
P.O. Box 719
Uhrichsville, Ohio 44683

1. Did you enjoy reading *Autumn Love*?
   ☐ Very much. I would like to see more books
      by this author!
   ☐ Moderately
      I would have enjoyed it more if _____

   _____

2. Are you a member of *Heartsong Presents*? Yes   No
   If no, where did you purchase this book? _____

   _____

3. What influenced your decision to purchase
   this book? (Circle those that apply.)

Cover	Back cover copy
Title	Friends
Publicity	Other _____

4. On a scale from 1 (poor) to 10 (superior), please rate the following elements.

    ___Heroine   ___Plot

    ___Hero   ___Inspirational theme

    ___Setting   ___Secondary characters

5. What settings would you like to see covered in *Heartsong Presents* books?

    _____

    _____

6. What are some inspirational themes you would like to see treated in future books?_____

    _____

    _____

7. Would you be interested in reading other *Heartsong Presents* titles?   Yes   No

8. Please circle your age range:

Under 18	18-24	25-34
35-45	46-55	Over 55

9. How many hours per week do you read? _____

Name _____

Occupation _____

Address _____

City _____ State _____ Zip _____

····· Hearts♥ng ·········

ROMANCE IS CHEAPER BY THE DOZEN!

Any 12 *Heartsong Presents* titles for only $26.95 *

Buy any assortment of twelve *Heartsong Presents* titles and save 25% off of the already discounted price of $2.95 each!

*plus $1.00 shipping and handling per order and sales tax where applicable.

HEARTSONG PRESENTS TITLES AVAILABLE NOW:

_HP 1 A TORCH FOR TRINITY, *Colleen L. Reece*
_HP 2 WILDFLOWER HARVEST, *Colleen L. Reece*
_HP 3 RESTORE THE JOY, *Sara Mitchell*
_HP 4 REFLECTIONS OF THE HEART, *Sally Laity*
_HP 5 THIS TREMBLING CUP, *Marlene Chase*
_HP 6 THE OTHER SIDE OF SILENCE, *Marlene Chase*
_HP 7 CANDLESHINE, *Colleen L. Reece*
_HP 8 DESERT ROSE, *Colleen L. Reece*
_HP 9 HEARTSTRINGS, *Irene B. Brand*
_HP10 SONG OF LAUGHTER, *Lauraine Snelling*
_HP11 RIVER OF FIRE, *Jacquelyn Cook*
_HP13 PASSAGE OF THE HEART, *Kjersti Hoff Baez*
_HP14 A MATTER OF CHOICE, *Susannah Hayden*
_HP15 WHISPERS ON THE WIND, *Maryn Langer*
_HP16 SILENCE IN THE SAGE, *Colleen L. Reece*
_HP17 LLAMA LADY, *VeraLee Wiggins*
_HP18 ESCORT HOMEWARD, *Eileen M. Berger*
_HP19 A PLACE TO BELONG, *Janelle Jamison*
_HP20 SHORES OF PROMISE, *Kate Blackwell*
_HP21 GENTLE PERSUASION, *Veda Boyd Jones*
_HP22 INDY GIRL, *Brenda Bancroft*
_HP23 GONE WEST, *Kathleen Karr*
_HP24 WHISPERS IN THE WILDERNESS, *Colleen L. Reece*
_HP25 REBAR, *Mary Carpenter Reid*
_HP26 MOUNTAIN HOUSE, *Mary Louise Colln*
_HP27 BEYOND THE SEARCHING RIVER, *Jacquelyn Cook*
_HP28 DAKOTA DAWN, *Lauraine Snelling*
_HP29 FROM THE HEART, *Sara Mitchell*
_HP30 A LOVE MEANT TO BE, *Brenda Bancroft*
_HP31 DREAM SPINNER, *Sally Laity*
_HP32 THE PROMISED LAND, *Kathleen Karr*
_HP33 SWEET SHELTER, *VeraLee Wiggins*
_HP34 UNDER A TEXAS SKY, *Veda Boyd Jones*
_HP35 WHEN COMES THE DAWN, *Brenda Bancroft*
_HP36 THE SURE PROMISE, *JoAnn A. Grote*
_HP37 DRUMS OF SHELOMOH, *Yvonne Lehman*
_HP38 A PLACE TO CALL HOME, *Eileen M. Berger*
_HP39 RAINBOW HARVEST, *Norene Morris*
_HP40 PERFECT LOVE, *Janelle Jamison*
_HP41 FIELDS OF SWEET CONTENT, *Norma Jean Lutz*

(If ordering from this page, please remember to include it with the order form.)

·········· Presents ··········

Great Inspirational Romance at a Great Price!

Heartsong Presents books are inspirational romances in contemporary and historical settings, designed to give you an enjoyable, spirit-lifting reading experience. You can choose from 64 wonderfully written titles from some of today's best authors like Colleen L. Reece, Brenda Bancroft, Janelle Jamison, and many others.

When ordering quantities less than twelve, above titles are $2.95 each.

LOVE A GREAT LOVE STORY?

Introducing Heartsong Presents —

Your Inspirational Book Club

Heartsong Presents Christian romance reader's service will provide you with four never before published romance titles every month! In fact, your books will be mailed to you at the same time advance copies are sent to book reviewers. You'll preview each of these new and unabridged books before they are released to the general public.

These books are filled with the kind of stories you have been longing for—stories of courtship, chivalry, honor, and virtue. Strong characters and riveting plot lines will make you want to read on and on. Romance is not dead, and each of these romantic tales will remind you that Christian faith is still the vital ingredient in an intimate relationship filled with true love and honest devotion.

Sign up today to receive your first set. Send no money now. We'll bill you only $9.97 post-paid with your shipment. Then every month you'll automatically receive the latest four "hot off the press" titles for the same low post-paid price of $9.97. That's a savings of 50% off the $4.95 cover price. When you consider the exaggerated shipping charges of other book clubs, your savings are even greater!

THERE IS NO RISK—you may cancel at any time without obligation. And if you aren't completely satisfied with any selection, return it for an immediate refund.

TO JOIN, just complete the coupon below, mail it today, and get ready for hours of wholesome entertainment.

Now you can curl up, relax, and enjoy some great reading full of the warmhearted spirit of romance.

— — Curl up with Heartsong! — —

YES! Sign me up for Heartsong!

NEW MEMBERSHIPS WILL BE SHIPPED IMMEDIATELY!
Send no money now. We'll bill you only $9.97 post-paid with your first shipment of four books. Or for faster action, call toll free 1-800-847-8270.

NAME _____

ADDRESS _____

CITY _____ STATE / ZIP _____

MAIL TO: HEARTSONG / P.O. Box 719 Uhrichsville, Ohio 44683
YES II